SKY REALM

SKY REALM

Crystal Doors, Book 3

REBECCA MOESTA
KEVIN J. ANDERSON

WFP
WORDFIRE PRESS

EBook ISBN: 978-1-68057-245-2
Trade Paperback ISBN: 978-1-68057-244-5

Cover design by Fantasy Book Design
Kevin J. Anderson, Art Director
Published by
WordFire Press, LLC
PO Box 1840
Monument CO 80132

Kevin J. Anderson & Rebecca Moesta, Publishers
WordFire Press eBook Edition 2021
WordFire Press Trade Paperback Edition 2021

Printed in the USA
Join our WordFire Press Readers Group for
sneak previews, updates, new projects, and giveaways.
Sign up at wordfirepress.com

DEDICATION

This book is for
SEAN MOORHEAD
a fellow traveler
to imaginary
and not-so-imaginary lands.

CHAPTER 1

Afresh ocean breeze blew through Gwen Pierce's baby-fine blond hair. In the distance below, the ocean surrounding Elantya sparkled a deep turquoise blue. Beneath her, the wondrous island city bustled with activity, as it had for the past week since she and her fellow apprentices had escaped captivity in the merlon king's undersea city. Up here in the sky, with buttery sunlight warming her skin, she felt safe. A few months ago she might have found the experience of riding a magic carpet unnerving, with nothing between her and a long drop to certain death other than a rectangle of purple cloth and a good friend. But she had changed.

Sharif had let her sit in front of him on the flying carpet today and, although it wasn't completely necessary, he kept one arm loosely around her waist to ensure that she would not fall. The billowing sleeves of the dark-haired prince's spotless white shirt rippled as he sailed his embroidered rug high above the harbor. Elantyan ships were anchored at intervals around the island, reinforcing its magical defenses.

Sharif leaned forward, pointing toward the horizon. "A storm is gathering far out at sea." From the corner of her eye, Gwen could see the prince's nymph djinni hovering above his shoulder in her eggsphere, shedding an electric green glow of anxiety on the dusky skin of his face.

"Piri does not think it is a magical storm," Sharif explained, "but she is not sure."

Looking out at the cluster of dark clouds, Gwen wished that she had no responsibilities and could stay in the air in peace and quiet all day long. But the wish lasted only for a moment. *Suck it up, Pierce*, she mentally scolded herself. *Let's see what you've got.* To Sharif, she said, "We should let the sages know about that bad weather."

Vic lowered his scroll and wiped away the sweat that streamed down his face. His throat felt raw. Beside him, Lyssandra kept reading aloud, though her voice came out in barely a whisper. They had been reciting spells for hours, standing together at the rail of the *Sea Child*, down the coast from the Elantyan harbor. The ship's deck moved beneath their feet. The hot sun beat down on them, warming the deck planks, reflecting off the waves, and making Vic's head throb with an ache that seemed to have gone on for days now. Pushing her long, coppery hair back from her elfin face, the petite girl unstoppered the vial of magically replenishing liquid she wore on a chain around her neck. She drank some of the healing greenstepe and offered it to Vic. He took several gulps and the throbbing in his head eased.

All around the ship, everyone with magical training—from novs to sages—also recited from various spell scrolls assigned to them by master sages. Each spell provided some measure of protection for the island, either in the form of a shield or a booby trap. Vic's spell temporarily disoriented any creature that ventured into the limited area it covered. Lyssandra's spell formed a swatch of invisible mesh. Ever since Vic and his fellow apprentices had escaped from the underwater city of Oo'regl a week ago, the entire island of Elantya had been a hub of frenetic activity. Students from the Citadel, regardless of their levels of competence, had been drafted by the sages to assist in reading spell scrolls. The work was time-consuming and exhausting, since the process had to be repeated again and again at hundreds of locations around the island. At least the leg wound Vic had gotten during their underwater escape no longer plagued him. Strong medical spells, administered first on the rescue ship and later in the Hall of Healers, had already returned him to full strength.

But the merlons were coming back, and the island had to be protected.

Sage Rubicas remained back in his laboratory, still working on expanding a shield spell that he hoped could eventually protect the entire island. The Pentumvirate put great faith in the snowy-bearded wizard—whose skills were a fusion of magic and science—and had recently named Rubicas the island's Ven Sage, the most powerful and respected bright sage in all Elantya. Entrusting the development of innovative armaments and protections to the workforce in the Ven Sage's chambers, the council of five leaders focused on directing the ongoing efforts to enhance security around the island. Vic's father, Cap Pierce, devoted most of his time to coordinating the various defense projects in Rubicas's lab. The rest of the former archaeology professor's waking hours were consumed with plans to rescue his wife—Vic's mother—from the ice coral cave in which the dark sage Azric had imprisoned her.

Alongside the ship, Tiaret, the girl from Afirik, surfaced from the depths and expertly blew water out of her lungs through her mouth and gills. When Rubicas's apprentices were kidnapped by the merlons, Azric's immortal henchman Orpheon had worked a spell to give all five of them gills. Because of this, Vic, Gwen, and their friends could still breathe underwater without assistance.

Steadying herself with her bare feet against the hull boards, Tiaret climbed a rope up to the deck. The dark-skinned girl was tall—almost as tall as Vic. Seawater sparkled on the lashes around her golden eyes and on the decorative bangles bound into the long, twisted strands of her dark brown hair. "Sage Polup reports that the removal of lavaja bombs from beneath the island is proceeding well, though more slowly than our anemonite friends had hoped." She unslung the teaching staff from her back. "Are we ready to move the ship to our next position?"

"Yup, just about," Vic said. "As soon as they get here." He pointed to the sky where a fluttering purple carpet descended toward the ship. The magic carpet carrying Sharif and Gwen swooped down to settle on the open deck. As soon as Vic's willowy cousin and the young man from Irrakesh jumped off, Sharif rolled the swatch of patterned purple fabric into a tidy cylinder, tucked it under his arm, and walked over to the closest sage to give a weather report.

"What's up, Doc?" Vic asked Gwen, using the name he had called his brainy cousin since they were kids.

"There's a storm as dark as blackstepe brewing out at sea." Gwen's dramatic violet eyes met her cousin's aquamarine gaze.

"Magical?" Vic asked, raising one eyebrow. "Merlon sorcery?"

"Piri does not think so," Sharif answered, returning from speaking to the sage. "But as my people say, 'No event is certain until it occurs.'"

Tiaret thumped the round end of her teaching staff on the

wooden deck. "That is why a story may not be entered in the Great Epic until *after* the events are complete."

"In other words, histories are more accurate than prophecies," Gwen said.

Vic glanced at Lyssandra, knowing that the girl's prophetic dreams rarely allowed her to sleep well. The petite telepath had dark circles beneath her cobalt-blue eyes.

She gave them all a wan smile. "It is precisely what I do not know that makes my visions so disturbing. Whether prophecies come in dreams or in words, they never seem to mean what they appear to say."

"The merlons had prophecies, too," Vic pointed out.

"Something about rage and merlon victory. I think they were interpreting them wrong—at least, I hope so—but I think Azric is behind that." Sweat prickled the scalp beneath his straight brown hair. He scratched his head. "Remind me again—*why* are merlons so set on destroying Elantya?"

Patiently, Lyssandra explained, "Because when the family of the dark sage Azric came through the crystal door to this world thousands of years ago, they were bent on conquering all worlds. After Azric betrayed and murdered his parents, he built up armies of immortal warriors in seven worlds. Bright sages from a dozen worlds joined together to create the island of Elantya at the center of all the doors, in order to prevent the dark sages and their followers from taking over."

"Although the merlons in this world did not grant their permission for this, neither did they object," Tiaret added.

Sharif's olive-green eyes were serious as he continued the tale. "After that, Azric's sister Aennia and the bright sage Qelsyn performed a great magic to seal the crystal doors to all worlds that held those immortal armies, but the magic was so strong that many other doors were sealed as well. Regrettably, Azric was not trapped behind any of the doors in the Great Closure.

Since then, he has traveled from world to world finding new followers to replace his lost armies."

"Fortunately for us, those new followers are not indestructible," Tiaret said.

Sharif's expression darkened. "Years ago Azric came in disguise to Irrakesh. My brother Hashim succeeded in exposing him and saving my people, but the dark sage killed him."

"For thousands of years after the Great Closing, Elantyans had no contact with merlons," Lyssandra said. "But all the while, Azric secretly gathered new supporters."

"And since he's come back to this world," Vic concluded, "the merlons suddenly want to murder every land-living creature. Coincidence? I think not." He thought of all the people he knew of who had been lost to Azric's insatiable desire to conquer.

"No coincidence, Taz," Gwen agreed, calling her cousin by the cartoon-inspired nickname she had given him when they were in kindergarten. "Azric wants the merlons to hate Elantya. He had no problems killing his own parents, and *mine*, and Sharif's brother—and who knows how many other thousands or millions of people who were in his way." Her violet eyes flashed with anger as she mentioned the dark sage. "And if everyone who can stop Azric is wiped out, he'll have all the time he needs to break the seals on those crystal doors."

"For that, he needs more than time, Doc. He needs us," Vic pointed out. He hesitated for a moment, then added, "Or my mom." Not only were Gwen and Vic the subjects of ancient prophecies about "Chosen Ones" and being "born beneath the selfsame moon," the cousins had inherited the rare gift of seal breaking from their mothers.

"What I do not understand," Lyssandra said, "is why the merlons hate people they do not know. It makes no sense to despise us simply because we live on land—or because Azric told them to hate us."

Just then, Piri hovered over the edge of the deck rail, blinking orange with alarm.

The apprentices looked down at the water and went silent with shock as something lithe and vaguely humanoid broke the surface just far enough away that it was not affected by the Elantyan protective spells. At the center of its forehead pulsed a pair of circular membranes. Fine green scales covered the creature's body, and huge, oily dark eyes flashed from the wide face. A lookout called from the tall mast. Others shouted, passing on the warning, and soon all magic users and sailors aboard crowded to the deck rail. Everyone on the ship knew exactly what they were seeing.

A merlon.

Tiaret brandished her teaching staff. Sages scrambled to find their most powerful spell scrolls. Burly sailors hauled out long harpoons.

The ugly thing in the water held up its webbed hands in a pacifying gesture. Without making a move toward the *Sea Child*, it looked up at the apprentices and made the loud garbled sounds of merlon speech.

Tiaret eyed the merlon warily, even though it seemed to be alone and unarmed.

"What did it say?" Vic asked Lyssandra, who could understand the speech of the aquatic race.

The telepathic girl looked at her friends in confusion. "He says his name is Ulbar. He asks that we take him to see our leaders."

CHAPTER 2

From the front row of benches in the nearly deserted rotunda of Elantya's Pentumvirate Hall, Vic, Gwen, and their friends watched the proceedings with interest. A smattering of colorfully garbed sages were also in the hall, along with all five members of the Pentumvirate, who had all hastily assembled to meet the unusual visitor from beneath the sea.

Tugging absently at his white beard, Ven Sage Rubicas read a translation scroll to make the merlon's speech comprehensible to everyone in the hall. Ulbar, who had a distinctive scarlet head fin, told an astonishing tale.

Gripping her teaching staff tightly, Tiaret eyed the aquatic visitor with suspicion. To her friends she muttered, "Are we to assume that peaceful merlons have truly shared this world with Elantya all along, yet the sages knew nothing of them?"

"Why not?" Vic answered in a low voice, so as not to interrupt Ulbar. "According to Ven Rubicas, the sages hardly had any contact with the merlons at all until the past century or so."

"As my people say—" Sharif began, but Gwen shushed them all.

"We need to hear all of what Ulbar says. Then we can decide if it's believable."

Vic was interested to see that several of the Virs, the leaders of Elantya's government, were gripping the rose and turquoise decision crystals on the arms of their stone chairs with apparent anxiety. None of them seemed to like being in the presence of this merlon. Vic certainly couldn't blame them. Come to think of it, he was feeling a bit queasy himself. So far, his experience with scaly people hadn't exactly been positive. Most members of the undersea race had either wanted to kill Vic or enslave him. Vic had also seen downtrodden merlon slaves, but he had considered them criminals, not peace-loving rebels, as Ulbar suggested.

Standing on the stone floor of the vaulted chamber, the merlon speaker seemed to squirm when Helassa asked, "Why should we believe you? If you are truly not among those merlons who for the past century have assaulted our ships, our island, and our people, the best that can be said of you is that you ignored our existence for millennia—even when Barak's merlons attacked us. How can you now expect us to trust you?" The Vir of Protection wore a Grecian-style gown of diaphanous crimson material. Her left hand rested on the decision crystal on her armrest. When lit, the turquoise crystal signified a Vir's negative vote on an issue.

Ulbar spread his webbed hands before the Pentumvirate. Though the spell allowed listeners to understand him, the merlon's speech still sounded raspy and bubbly, as if his gills were full of phlegm. "We were at peace. Your presence did not affect us, nor did your war with distant Oo'regl. Your ships rarely travel past the boundary of crystal doors in this world, and we live far outside that circle. Safe. As chieftain of the city of Oo'sqibl, I felt that any disagreement between you and King

Barak—half a world away from us—was irrelevant to my citizens."

At this, white-robed Etherya gave a faint smile. Vic had heard that the Vir of Arts was a great-grandmother already, but Etherya's dark hair and clear voice made her seem much younger. "And are the people of Elantya now relevant?"

Ulbar took a slithery step backward and bowed his head slightly. "King Barak and Azric have made you relevant." The members of the Pentumvirate exchanged glances as the merlon went on. "I believe that Azric chose to corrupt those merlons that live closest to this island. Recently, Barak has become increasingly power mad. He began demanding tribute from cities that are far from his realm. He sent dark sages and an army against Oo'nisl and Oo'beebl, capturing many innocent merlons who opposed him. Even when Barak enslaved the chieftains of those cities, I and the more distant chieftains said nothing. *We* were safe, so it did not concern us. But now … Several days ago, a weary and tortured anemonite came to my city of Oo'sqibl. We fed and sheltered her and her kraega steed, and in return, she told us her story. She said several young land-dwellers had helped her people to escape Oo'regl, where King Barak had held them all captive. She explained King Barak's plan to destroy everyone on Elantya, as well as his pledge to help the dark sage Azric in his quest to unseal the crystal doors and unleash his deathless armies on all the worlds."

"And that is what brought you here?" asked Questas, the blue-robed Vir of Learning. "You need our help?"

"I propose an alliance." Again, Ulbar bowed his head, as if in shame. "Two days ago, General Goldskin arrived in my city with a ruthless band of merlon warriors. She told us that Azric has left this world to gather his loyal followers through other crystal doors to join with King Barak in a great battle against Elantya. Goldskin demanded five hundred of my strongest warriors to join in Barak's 'holy cause' of ridding Szishh of all land-dwellers. She warned if we did not fight beside them, they would return to destroy Oo'sqibl once their victory was complete. They would slaughter every adult merlon and take our children as slaves."

In alarm, Helassa rose halfway from her stone chair.

Ulbar did not flinch, though he hastened to add, "To my great honor, every one of my warriors swam with me in rejecting Goldskin's demand. We drove her forces from Oo'sqibl. Barak and his armies have listened to false prophets. Their cause is not holy, and they will cause many deaths. Alas, they have coerced other tribes to fight beside them. Barak and his minions are your enemies. They are our enemies. We can fight together to defeat them while we protect as many good merlons as possible." His fins fluttered and extended in a glorious, thorny frill. "It is the only honorable way we can free all merlons from the influence of an evil king and the evil sage."

"How could you help us?" Vir Parsimanias asked in clipped syllables. The yellow-clad Vir of Resources showed interest in anything that could benefit Elantya.

Vic saw Ulbar's ugly, earnest face relax as some of the tension flowed out of it. "Then you agree to an alliance? We will help you in your struggles to safeguard your citizens, this island, and all of the crystal door worlds if you, in turn, pledge to help me protect my people." Ulbar's scarlet head fin rippled as he thought for a moment before he then said, "We can assist your anemonites in locating the remaining lavaja bombs in the catacombs Barak's people created beneath your island. We can post scouts underwater around your island. I will also send a few of my most trusted men to Goldskin to pretend that they have deserted our city and wish to fight with Barak's army. My men can send us word when the forces of Oo'regl plan to attack."

Helassa's deep indigo eyes narrowed. "Or perhaps your plan is to infiltrate Elantya while posing as our friends. And then, when the battle with Barak's merlons begins, you will turn against us and defeat us from within."

"Classic strategy," Vic whispered to his friends.

Ulbar stiffened at Helassa's accusation, then seemed to force himself to calm down. His colorful fins retracted. "It is true that our people have no reason to trust one another. Merlons have attacked your ships, and humans have killed many merlons. The anemonite warned us that this would be so. Therefore, we brought the anemonite with us so that you may verify what I have said. We also brought a peace offering. If Azric were to learn what we have stolen from him, he would destroy Oo'sqibl down to the last minnow." He turned slowly, blinking his lamp-like eyes at the hushed listeners in the rotunda. "To receive this gift, I ask that you come with me to the harbor."

Ripples from the approaching thunderstorm made the harbor waters choppy. The assemblage from the Pentumvirate Hall gathered on the shore.

"What do you think he brought, Doc?" Vic said to his cousin. "What if it's a sea serpent? Wouldn't that be cool?"

She gave him one of her please-grow-up looks. "You would think so."

Not far away, Vic's father and Sage Polup tested several new weapons, including an improved version of the anemonite scientist's Grogyptian Fire cannon.

At the merlon ambassador's request, the wary Virs had temporarily dropped some of the defensive spells at the mouth of the harbor. Doctor Pierce and the jellyfish scientist were ready to respond with force, however, if the merlon showed any sign of treachery.

At the edge of the water, Ulbar raised his hands without

further ceremony, summoning his comrades to deliver the mysterious "gift." Not far from the end of the docks, the water began to churn and bubble with activity. Moments later, the head of another merlon broke the surface. Then another and another, until there were at least a score of the aquatic people swimming slowly toward the shallows.

Gwen gave an involuntary gasp of alarm, but soon everyone could see the jellyfish-like anemonite scientist on her kraega steed leading them. Dripping and hissing as they emerged into the air, the merlons guided something large and vaguely human shaped. When they were waist-deep in the water, the merlons parted ranks. Ulbar splashed into the water to draw attention to the priceless peace offering they had brought.

A beautiful, delicate form, enveloped in an impenetrable cocoon of ice coral.

Vic called out while, with a strangled cry, his father ran forward.

"Mom!"

"Kyara!"

CHAPTER 3

E ven on an island of wonder and magic, the main chamber of Rubicas's laboratory held more marvels than a pair of highly curious teenagers could absorb. The walls, floors, and soaring columns of the broad, oval chamber were made of richly veined, polished marble. Prismatic skylights that encircled the lofty central dome let in plentiful daylight. Sun crystals embedded in the ceiling—laid out in the patterns of constellations—charged themselves by day and glowed at night to allow work to continue at all hours. Shelves overflowed with spell scrolls and supplies for experiments, both magical and scientific. In Elantya, magic and science were cousins, as close as Gwen and Vic.

The great experimental chamber was crowded with sages, neosages, journeysages, apprentices, and novs, as well as anemonite scientists who had escaped the merlons with Lyssandra. Around the room, they clustered at experiments and defense projects in various stages of completion. In the gear-up to defend against Barak's merlons, some eager workers were assigned to help Ven Sage Rubicas expand his shield spell. Others aided Lyssandra's father Groxas in his pyrosage duties. The rest helped Vic's father prepare cannons, catapults, sunshine bombs, handheld arrowpults tipped with crystals of fire aja, and undersea equipment, for land and sea battles. During breaks, Dr. Pierce had also been planning a rescue mission for his wife, but now that Ulbar's merlons had brought her back, he would start working on a means of reviving her.

Seawater aquariums lined the curved walls from floor to ceiling. The massive tanks were home to all manner of ocean life—colorful electric eels, strobe snails, multihued plants—and aquits, the small shape-shifting messengers of the sea, which reminded Vic and Gwen of doll-sized mermaids. But no tank anywhere in Elantya had ever held as exotic a treasure as the one beside which the twin cousins now stood with their friends and Ven Rubicas. From the head of the reservoir that held Kyara Pierce's ice coral-entrapped form, Vic's father watched over his wife while Ven Rubicas read from yet another spell scroll.

Vic couldn't tear his eyes away from his mother. A xyridium pendant, identical to those that he and Gwen wore, hung on a fine chain around her neck. Kyara's long dark hair seemed to float beneath her head, and her eyes were closed, as if in sleep. Dressed in a gown of filmy green layers, she looked like an enchanted princess from a fairy tale.

"S'ibah," the Ven Sage ended in a whisper. "Hmm. That should keep the seawater circulating until we find a way to free her."

"We didn't know we would have to keep her in seawater to maintain the preservation spell," Vic's father said.

Gwen said, "According to Azric, releasing her all at once from the ice coral would be fatal. We've got to find some other way."

Vic's father swallowed hard and shook his head in dismay. "If Ulbar hadn't told us, I might have made a mistake and injured Kyara." His face twisted into a mask of grief and guilt. *Or worse.*

"She is safe for now, Sage Pierce," Lyssandra said quietly.

Vic knew his telepathic friend was only trying to comfort them, but he could not keep the bitterness from his voice. "*Safe?* You mean like Sleeping Beauty was safe in a crystal coffin?" The copper-haired girl placed her hand on his arm to draw the unfamiliar reference from his mind. She winced as she understood his meaning.

"But Sleeping Beauty wasn't dead, Taz," Gwen pointed out gently. "And neither is your mom. If only waking her up were as easy as a kiss."

A wild look of hope stole into Dr. Pierce's eyes a split second before he plunged his head face first into the water and pressed his lips to the ice coral above his wife's mouth. Although Vic and his friends could breathe under water because of the gill spell Orpheon had cast on them, Dr. Pierce could not.

Vic's father stood up straight. Water streamed down his face. "I had to try. No idea is too crazy. We can't give up."

"Hmm," Ven Rubicas said, inspecting Kyara's frozen form.

"If your method had succeeded, we would have seen some result by now."

Vic put an arm around his father's wet shoulders. "It's okay, Dad. We'll find a way. We knew it would take some time." Vic was an optimist, but he could understand how his father felt: he was so close—right here with the person he had been dreaming about seeing again for years—and yet unable to talk to Kyara, to touch her. Vic's mother probably wasn't even aware of their presence. And, if they did not come up with a solution, she might remain a beautiful statue permanently.

Sharif leaned closer to Vic. "It is possible that the Air Spirits of Irrakesh would know how to save your mother." To Vic's surprise, Piri glowed white with pride and then red with anger, then alternated between the two. "No, Piri," the prince assured his small friend. "Even though I turned my back on them, I would never ask the Air Spirits to grant a wish and drain their life force."

Piri's glow turned to a deep blue of sadness.

Just then, a large wine-red magic carpet twice the size of Sharif's purple one sailed through one of the arched open windows of the chamber and glided to the floor beside the tank. A middle-aged man with dark skin and a red turban rose smoothly to his feet from a cross-legged position on the rug.

Sharif started to greet the new arrival, but the man gave a sad shake of his head and made a formal announcement. "I have news for Prince Ali el Sharif from his father, His Most Exalted Majesty, the Sultan of Irrakesh. As of this moment, the prince is no longer a student at the Citadel. The sultan commands his son to return to Irrakesh immediately."

CHAPTER 4

The hot mineral water that steamed and bubbled around the five friends did not soothe and relax Gwen as it usually did. Instead, it reminded her that her life was changing once again, and apparently there was nothing she could do about it. The sultan's messenger had departed immediately, giving Sharif only one day to gather his things, say his goodbyes, and wrap up any uncompleted business at the Citadel. The prince would have to return home.

Gwen had no more control over this situation than she'd had when Azric had murdered her parents, or when she'd gone to live with Uncle Cap and Vic, or when she and her cousin had been thrown through a crystal door to this strange world, or when the merlons had attacked them aboard the *Golden Walrus*, or when she and Vic had found out that they were the subjects of some mysterious prophecy. And on and on. It seemed she was never in full control. Gwen touched the five-sided medallion on its thong around her neck and thought of how so many unpleasant and confusing circumstances had been thrust upon her and Vic. And now Sharif had no choice, either.

The young man from Irrakesh sat close to her in the hot springs pool at the center of the apprentices' living area, gripping her hand tightly, as if he thought she could keep him here in Elantya. Piri hovered close to his face in her eggsphere, glowing a sunny yellow and trying to cheer him up by rolling her sphere up his cheek and down the center of his nose. But Sharif would not be comforted.

"You do not wish to go home," Tiaret said. A statement, not a question.

"No, I do not. In Irrakesh, the second son of a sultan is of little consequence. My kind and wise brother Hashim should have been the next sultan. My father doted on him, and after Hashim's death my father could scarcely bear to look at me. When I asked to come to the Citadel to study, he seemed relieved and told me it would be a good many years before he would call upon me for any duty. Even my sisters were more important to him, since they had been married away to form alliances with other powerful families."

Gwen sat bolt upright in the water. "You have sisters?"

Sharif nodded. "Seven of them. All are grown and married already, but Naima and Zari—the two who still lived at the palace when Hashim was murdered—comforted my father, and he felt no need for me to stay. I was released from any court obligations, so I came to Elantya to study."

"Like *The Student Prince*," Gwen said, remembering the old musical her father had liked to listen to.

"And now I am ordered home at my father's whim," Sharif said, "no doubt to begin serious training to become sultan many years from now. A responsibility for which I have absolutely no desire."

Vic gave Sharif a look of commiseration. "Peter Pan didn't want to grow up, either."

Lyssandra touched Vic's arm and gave a sad smile as she

drew the thought from his mind. "I am not certain any one of us wishes for that, yet we grow up by need, not by choice."

"So it is in the Great Epic," Tiaret pointed out. "I have not been a child since the Grassland Wars." Her teaching staff lay at the edge of the hot springs pool, and she gripped it with one hand as if to emphasize that she might be called upon to defend them at a moment's notice. "And you, my friends, have battled the merlons and seen betrayal and death. Your names are already written in the Great Epic. You cannot cling to your child-hoods. The prophecies—"

"Of course. The prophecies!" Vic said, slapping the surface of the bubbling water and sending a hot splash into all of their faces. "Lyssandra, didn't you say we're all part of the prophecy in that children's song? Sing it for us."

"The fingerplay? Of course." Lyssandra said the rhyme, adding the hand movements that went with each part.

Raised from deep beneath the ocean, Five required to be complete,
Prophecies are set in motion, Leaving evil no retreat.
Forming bonds from worlds divergent, Pledged to serve and to protect,
At the time when need is urgent, Ancient powers intersect.

Vic listened, fidgeting with his medallion. "See, Doc? *Five* required to be complete."

"So if all of us are in the prophecy," Gwen concluded, "then we need Sharif here to help us fight Azric. We can't just let him go back to Irrakesh and stay there."

Piri twinkled an optimistic aqua, and cautious hope lit Sharif's eyes. But the hope died away as quickly as it had flared. "No, my father will not believe that. He believes his needs—and those of Irrakesh—are more important. The other prophecies speak only of the two of you who are needed to create a Ring of Might that can defeat Azric."

Gwen, whose heart had leapt with joy at the idea that Sharif might be allowed to stay, denied this. "Prophecies don't always mean what you think they mean," she pointed out. "What if we can't do this without your help?"

"Sheesh, that reminds me," Vic said. "I came up with a theory about that whole Ring of Might thing last night. Something Lyssandra told us about one of her dreams got me to thinking—kind of in the Scotty-only-has-three-hours-to-fix-the-Enterprise-before-everybody-gets-blown-up sort of way. I knew Azric and the merlons would be coming, and somehow it just popped into my head."

Hoping that her cousin had found a solution to their current dilemma, Gwen found herself becoming impatient for him to get to the point. "In other words…?"

"In other words, Doc, I think we've had enough hints now." He pointed to the medallion at his neck. "Where did I used to keep this?"

"As a fob on your keychain," she said immediately.

Vic sighed with exasperation. "Well, *we're* all Keys, aren't we —the five of us?" Without waiting for an answer, he plunged on. "And I used to keep my medallion on a key *ring*, not a keychain."

"So …" Gwen began.

"So this Ring of Might you and I are supposed to forge isn't the snatch-it-from-Gollum-and-toss-it-into-the-Cracks-of-Doom kind of ring."

Gwen's heart skipped a beat as the truth of his words sank in. "The Ring we're supposed to forge is a Key Ring? The five of us, right here."

Vic gave her an eyebrow shrug. "I'll take Misunderstood Prophecies for a thousand, Alex."

"You're right. We've been forging that Ring for months now," Gwen said. "And it's up to us to make sure that it stays together and is strong enough to stop Azric."

"His plan is to unseal the doors, reunite his immortal armies, and conquer all worlds." Tiaret looked at Sharif with somber golden eyes. "If he should succeed, Irrakesh too will be in grave danger. Perhaps if we explained to your father—"

"No," Gwen said, "as the children of the prophecy, it's Vic's and my responsibility to forge the Ring and to make certain it stays together."

"We could all go to Irrakesh," Lyssandra suggested. "That is another way we could all remain together."

Vic's mouth fell open and his aquamarine eyes glowed with enthusiasm. "Sheesh, of course, why didn't I think of that? Sharif, didn't you say that the Air Spirits of Irrakesh might have the power to help my mom?"

Piri's sphere flickered orange with worry.

"Yes, but—" Sharif began. Gwen wondered if the prince was reluctant to let them meet his stern-sounding father.

Just then, a concussion seemed to rock Rubicas's entire laboratory building with a sound like sonic booms striking a thousand brass cymbals. The water in the hot springs sloshed wildly and splashed out all over the stone floor. By the time Gwen blinked and wiped the water from her eyes, Tiaret had already sprung from the pool and was racing toward the stairs that led up to the experimental chamber, her teaching staff in hand. The rest of the friends scrambled out and followed, wearing only their swim brevis and not bothering to dry off.

When they slid to a stop at the top of the stairs from the underground chamber, the entire room was in an uproar. Water had sploshed from the aquariums and from Kyara's preservation tank, where Cap was feverishly checking the tank and ice coral for any damage. A large, jagged crack ran across the smooth marble floor. And pyrosage Groxas was lying flat on his back beside Ven Sage Rubicas's high stool and marble lectern.

"Is everyone safe?" Rubicas asked in a loud voice.

Lyssandra hurried over to check on her father, who brushed smoldering embers from his bushy black beard. While Tiaret scanned the room for enemies, Sharif checked the aquariums, and Gwen and Vic slipped and slid their way over to Kyara's tank.

"Nothing serious this time," Dr. Pierce answered Rubicas, "but that must not happen again. It could kill Kyara!"

Lyssandra helped her father sit up.

"A minor miscalculation," Sage Groxas said. "I was attempting to denature one of the aja bombs that the merlons planted beneath the island. Ven Rubicas covered it with his most powerful shield spell before I read from my pyro neutralization scroll. It should have worked."

"Hmm," Rubicas said, tugging thoughtfully at his snowy white beard. "Henceforth, we will have to relocate these experiments to a less populated area of the island without buildings." He got down from his high stool, went to a shelf, and rummaged for a spell scroll.

Groxas indicated a small crater that the explosion had left in the floor. "As you can see, the result was not what I expected."

Rubicas read his spell scroll over the crater and said, "*S'ibah.*" The cracks and roughness in the broken rock began to blur and flow together to fill in the damaged area. While the destruction was healing itself, the apprentices explained Vic's Key Ring theory to the sages—as well as the suggestion that the Air Spirits might be able to offer advice about restoring Kyara—and asked permission to accompany Sharif.

Rubicas cracked his knuckles. "Hmm. Yes, that might prove quite useful."

Uncle Cap's eyes were bright with new hope as he looked at Gwen, then Vic. "Yes, go to Irrakesh. See if you can help your mother."

"And Elantya," Rubicas added.

CHAPTER 5

Early the next morning, Ven Sage Rubicas, Sage Pierce, and Vir Questas accompanied the apprentices to the docks, where they would board a ship that would take them to the crystal door that led to Irrakesh. The weather was fine and clear and not at all befitting the sadness of the occasion for Sharif.

The distress of having to leave Elantya surprised Sharif with its strength. The Elantyan port was alive with activity, with everyone going about their business preparing for war with the merlons. Just like any other day. Like a bodyguard, Tiaret strode beside the prince, using her teaching staff as a walking stick.

A few steps ahead of them, Vic joked with his cousin and Lyssandra. None of them seemed the least bit worried about this trip to Irrakesh. Perhaps they were confident that they could convince the sultan to let Sharif return to Elantya. Whatever the reason, it was obvious that no one's heart was as heavy as his.

A musical voice spoke in his mind, *Good friends*, Piri said. *Love you.*

During her time in the searing lavaja, the nymph djinni had

learned to communicate somewhat, though so far she had only spoken to Sharif. Her glowing sphere hovered next to his cheek to comfort him.

When they reached their ship, the *Song of Therya*, Ven Sage Rubicas read a spell scroll that would speed the trireme on its way out to the crystal door. Sage Pierce hugged each of the apprentices and gave Vic and Gwen several pieces of typically parental advice—"Trust your instincts," and "Be polite. Remember, you're guests in a strange culture," and "Stay safe"—the sort of things Sharif's father had never bothered to tell him. The two sages bade everyone farewell and returned to the laboratory, but Vir Questas, to everyone's surprise, volunteered to accompany the ship as far as the crystal door.

When they all boarded the ship, Tiaret and Gwen began nibbling on bits of shinqroot to settle their stomachs for the voyage. As the *Song of Therya* pulled away from the dock and headed out of the harbor, Tiaret challenged her fellow apprentices to a group sparring match on the open deck. Sharif declined. Still not ready to let go of the island, he went to the stern rail to look at Elantya. Gwen joined him. She seemed to sense that he didn't want to talk, and they gazed across the water in companionable silence. It was good to have a friend nearby at times like this. He wished he could just stay on the island.

He felt torn. What did he have to complain about? He had enjoyed the carefree life of a prince and the freedom of doing all that he wished to do. He had been spoiled. On the other hand, because he knew that his mother and brother were dead, and that his father and sisters thought little about him, he had come to think of Elantya as the home of his heart. This was where he had met people who accepted him as a friend—not for his title or his wealth, but because they genuinely cared about him whether he was prince in another land, a student in Elantya, or a slave in the merlon city of Oo'regl.

And in that captivity beneath the sea, he had learned about the true wealth he possessed: the magic carpet with its semi-sentient dogged loyalty; his education at the Citadel from gifted sages from a hundred different worlds; the wisdom of his people that had sustained him as he remembered their insightful sayings, both in good times and in bad; the friendship his fellow apprentices had bestowed on him; and the unconditional love of Piri, who had been willing to sacrifice her very life to save him under the sea. How glad he was that she had survived and been strengthened by the magical aja!

How could he have learned or experienced even half as much if he had stayed home in Irrakesh? It wasn't that Sharif didn't care about his people. He cared more than ever. Now that he recognized how truly wealthy he was, even without gold or jewels or palaces or servants, he felt the clear obligation to fight evil and keep his people safe.

In fact, he felt responsible for more than just his people. At one time he'd been unable to face the sheer boredom and drudgery of being tied down to one city on one world, to watch over the common people who were so far beneath him. Now he could not imagine staying there, but for a different reason: it would be selfish to let himself be sheltered and pampered while world after world fell to Azric and his power-hungry minions. If he truly had a special gift and was a member of the Ring of Might, as Vic believed, it was Sharif's duty to protect all people —to stand against Azric and his armies and defeat them, even if it meant that Sharif might die in the process.

New you, Piri observed. *Different now. Show Sultan.*

"You're right, Piri," he replied. "I'll have to make him understand."

Gwen found herself wondering why the Vir of Learning had decided to accompany them on this short trip. When the blue-robed Questas gathered the apprentices at midday to speak privately with him, his wise face was grave. "Viccus and Gwenya, do you believe that you are the children of the prophecy?"

Vic scratched his nose. "Yup. It looks that way. We weren't totally convinced at first, but—"

"The evidence is pretty overwhelming," Gwen finished for him. "First, we were born under the same moon, like in the prophecy Lyssandra is always quoting."

At Gwen's cue, the copper-haired telepath recited,

Born beneath the selfsame moon,

Only they may bind the rune,

And create the Ring of Might,

Right the wrongs, reverse the rite.

Gwen nodded and held up two fingers. "Second, Vic's father and mine were identical twins and our mothers were sisters, so our blood is really the same. That's part of another prophecy that starts with 'Brothers twin and sisters twain.'"

"Eighth," Vic interrupted, trying to throw her off track, as he often did.

She punched his arm. "Third," she went on, putting up a third finger, "these medallions we wear are made of xyridium, which isn't found anywhere on Earth. Neither is the design. The question is, are the medallions part of the Big Plan, whatever that is? I get the feeling this pattern could be the 'rune' in the prophecy. Fourth, Azric is convinced that we're the children of the prophecy, and he's had five thousand years to think about it, and—"

"Umpteenth," Vic put in.

"Fifth, if Taz is right and we manage to forge this Ring of Might among the five of us, there won't be any doubt left at all."

Vir Questas ran a thoughtful gaze around the circle. "How did you first recognize the special connection you all have?"

"We always knew we made a good team," Vic answered immediately, "but it didn't really sink in until the day we were tested as Keys together."

"Yes," Lyssandra agreed, thinking back. "Sharifas and I already knew we were potential Keys, but Tiaretya, Gwenya, and Viccus had yet to be tested."

"Our crystals lit, proving that we were Keys," Tiaret went on. "*All* of our crystals—all five at once."

Piri, who was resting lightly on Sharif's shoulder, seemed to burn with a bright yellow-white fire at the memory.

"And even more strangely," Sharif said, "the crystals continued to glow brighter and brighter."

Vic smiled. "Sheesh, with the way all the people in the Crystal Doors Center reacted, you would've thought we just created a lake on Dune—uh, in the desert, that is."

"It was as foretold in the prophecy," Lyssandra said.

Crystals five will shine like suns,
Thus reveal the Chosen Ones.
When the learning time is done,
Chosen Ones may choose as one,
Heralding the final fight,
Sages Dark with Sages Bright.

"Vir Pecunyas said it had never happened before," Gwen said.

"Yes," Vir Questas said. "I recall that he was most impressed. That incident was what first convinced him there was more to your small group than met the eye. There are those on our council, however—Helassa and Parsimanias—who do not believe that children, for that is how they see you, can have any significant role to play in saving Elantya from Azric. But Virs Etherya and Pecunyas and I are of a different mind. It was at their request that I came on this voyage, in the hopes that I could help you in whatever small way."

"Parsimanias and Helassa, huh?" Vic said with a frown. "That explains a lot already."

"And so, children of the prophecy, with dire times approaching, now would be an excellent time to forge that Ring of Might."

Vic groaned. "But didn't that one prophecy say 'when the learning time is done'? We're nowhere close to knowing everything we need to know."

"It seems that *my* learning time may be done," Sharif pointed out.

"True," Lyssandra said. "The prophecy was not specific about whose learning time."

Vic slapped himself on the forehead. "Sheesh. Every time you think you know what a prophecy means, another part of it sneaks up on you like that."

Gwen nibbled at the edge of her lower lip. "I've been thinking. Taz, you remember when you and I were trying to open a crystal door to Earth? We went to the Cogitarium, studied spell scrolls, and collected a variety of ingredients, including star aja." She looked guiltily at Vir Questas. "I'm still sorry that we ruined two of your crystals."

"It was the doing of that traitorous Orpheon," Sharif growled.

"You were attempting to increase your knowledge," Vir Questas said, "so I cannot object too greatly."

Gwen nodded. "Still, I'm sorry. Anyway, you wrote a spell, Taz, and we set up the crystals, and we measured and remeasured and—"

"And your point is?" Vic broke in.

"My point is the two of us worked *magic*," Gwen said. "We decided to do something, and we tried, and we did it—well, almost."

"I still don't grok what you're saying, Doc," Vic said.

"I mean, Vir Questas is right. It's time for us to forge the Ring of Might, and we can't just wait for something to happen. We've got to figure out how to do it ourselves."

Piri twinkled her encouragement, and Sharif translated. "My friend reminds me that my people have a saying, 'Make no wish unless you follow it with action.'"

Vic shrugged one shoulder. "Sure, I'm game. Maybe we should stand in sort of a circle or pentagon, since it worked so well when we took the Key test."

Vic and Gwen shut their eyes and concentrated.

Nothing happened.

"Are you really focusing?" Gwen whispered to her cousin.

"Maybe we need a spell," Vic suggested.

Gwen was relieved. "Of course. Maybe some crystals would help, too."

Vir Questas, watching from beside them, said, "Alas, I have no star aja to offer you this time."

"I have a crystal, however," Tiaret said, pulling her dagger from a fold of her animal skin outfit. "We all received them from Vir Helassa herself."

Sharif pulled his from the pocket of his pantaloons and held it up.

"Cool," Vic said, producing his crystal dagger. Lyssandra and Gwen did the same.

"Okay," Gwen said, "now hold your dagger in your right hand, then clasp hands with the person next to you around the hilt." She faced her cousin with a serious look in her dramatic violet eyes. "This is important, Taz. We can't just 'attempt' to do it. We have to actually *do* it."

Vic gave her a cheeky grin. "You're preaching to the choir, Yoda. There is no try."

This time when the cousins closed their eyes and concentrated, Gwen felt a difference right away, a spark, a current going through her. She opened her eyes. The crystal daggers they all held blazed a brilliant yellow. Piri's eggsphere sparkled yellow in response. The flow grew stronger, shivering and tickling through Gwen's entire body. Her scalp prickled. The xyridium medallions around Gwen's and Vic's necks began to glow as well, and they hovered into the air until the five-sided pendants floated flat and parallel to the ground just beneath the cousins' chins.

She wasn't sure why, but each corner on the two pendants pointed to one of the apprentices.

Without warning, Vic spoke.

"Forging five into one band,
Five become the Ring of Might,
Joining to protect the land,
And empowered to fight the fight."

She hadn't known her cousin was going to say anything— much less recite what sounded like a spell—and judging by his expression, he was just as surprised as she. As if they had coordinated it, the moment Vic stopped speaking, Gwen said, "*S'ibah.*"

Aquamarine lightning bolts shot from the edges of Vic's pendant and connected to each crystal in the group. Likewise, Gwen's pendant shot out violet fire. Beside her, Sharif gasped as the magical net increased the power flowing through the group by tenfold. Sparkling silver and gold strands finer than a spider's web spread from the point of each dagger and linked to the tips of the other four daggers in the group. Her concentration focused entirely within their circle, and she could not see the ship, the sky, the ocean, or Vir Questas. The hairs on the back of

Gwen's neck stood on end. Tingling ripples ran from the soles of her feet to the top of her scalp and back down, and she could feel herself linked, not just to Vic, but to Sharif, Lyssandra, and Tiaret as well, in a way she had never felt before.

The power built and built. A glowing design identical to the one on their medallions burned in the air at the center of the circle. Piri moved her sphere to hover directly above it. A few slender lightning jolts shot out and struck the eggsphere, reflected from it, and bounced back to the rune at the center again. Even the slave brand on Sharif's upper arm seemed to radiate a pure fire.

Gwen felt simultaneously tiny and enormous, powerful and powerless, ecstatic and tortured. An unbearable tension built inside her until she could hold it in no longer. At the same moment, as if with one voice, every one of the apprentices let out a shout.

"S'ibah!"

Gwen blinked. What had just happened? The dancing webs of electricity were gone, but the bond that linked them all to each other was strong. Instinctively she understood that the Ring of Might had been forged. She wasn't quite sure what the Ring's powers were, but she and her cousin—the children of the prophecy—had worked the magic.

"Cool," Vic said.

Gwen stared at Vic. "So where did that spell come from, Taz?"

He gave her an eyebrow shrug. "Trust me, I'm as surprised as you are. It, uh, just kinda popped out."

She chuckled. "In other words, you're telling me that just blurting out the first thing that pops into your head is actually a magical power now?"

"Come on, Doc. Group hug now, analyze magic later."

Vir Questas approached the apprentices with a look of

amazement. "You must be hungry," he said, setting down a large tray of food, and Gwen found that she was. Ravenous. It was no longer midday as it had been when they had formed their circle. The sun was setting.

"How … long?" Lyssandra asked as they all released hands and put away the crystal daggers.

"Ah. You have been here at least six hours, veiled in a mystical vapor," Questas said. "The sailors were alarmed at first, but I sensed the nature of the mist and reassured them that a wondrous event was taking place."

Remaining in their circle, they all sat around the food tray and helped themselves to cups of greenstepe, mugs of cool mos ale, and thick chunks of heavy brown bread covered with slabs of cheese. Every muscle in Gwen's body ached, and as she helped herself to the food, she couldn't remember ever tasting anything as delicious as this simple fare. While they refreshed themselves, the Vir explained that he believed new powers were now active in each member of the Ring and that they must try to discover them and learn how to use them.

"And now," he said, "it is time for you to take your leave. We arrived at the crystal door an hour ago. It is time to open it."

"No problem," Vic said, reading the unlocking rune Azric had tattooed on his wrist. He spoke the words that the dark sage had taught them, and the air began to sparkle with crystalline fire in the shape of an enormous arch on the water as the door opened.

"I had meant for Sharifas to unlock it," Questas said with surprise. "This is his world."

"I have never opened one before," Sharif said.

"Then you should," Tiaret said, making a throwing motion with both hands. A heartbeat later, the crystal door was gone.

Gwen stared in shock. Crystal doors usually stayed open for

a few minutes, yet this one had disappeared in a matter of seconds.

"What did you do?" Vic asked his friend from Afirik.

Tiaret spread her hands as if the answer were obvious. "I closed the door so that the prince could practice opening it."

Gwen bit the edge of her lower lip. "So the question is —*how*? Azric never taught us that."

Tiaret frowned with thought. "I do not know how. I wanted the door to close, and it closed."

"In other words," Gwen said, "you have a new skill. Now that we've forged the Ring of Might, you can slam crystal doors shut the moment you want to."

Their eyes all turned to Vir Questas, who nodded. "I have never seen this skill practiced before, but there are legends. The skill could be of great value in defending Elantya against those who would do us harm." He handed Sharif a small spell scroll.

Facing where the crystal door should be, Sharif read the spell and the doorway appeared again.

Gwen concentrated and tried to shut the glittering portal, but nothing happened. Vic, Sharif, and Lyssandra made the attempt, too, but to no avail.

"Can you still close it?" Gwen asked Tiaret, wanting to make sure they had more than one data point in their experiment of finding the Ring's new powers. An eyeblink later, Gwen had her answer. The door was gone.

Sharif stepped forward and read the spell scroll again. By the time he and Tiaret had opened and closed the door several times, everyone was convinced, and the girl from Afirik was tiring noticeably. Apparently, non-scroll magic took a certain amount of energy from those who used it.

"I am ready now. Ready to go home," Sharif said. He hesitated. "There is something I must ask of my friends before we travel to my city. Since Hashim's death, my father permits no one to bring weapons into the palace. Would it bother you greatly to leave them behind?"

"Not a problem," Vic said, getting his crystal knife out again and handing it to Questas. The others gave him theirs, as well, but Tiaret was reluctant to give up her teaching staff.

The blue-robed Vir gently put a hand out for it. "I will keep this safe for you until you return."

"Please?" Sharif said. "I promise to take care of you while you are in Irrakesh."

With a troubled look, the warrior girl relinquished the staff to Vir Questas.

"Thank you, my friends," the prince said with a look of relief. Then, reading from the spell scroll, he opened the door again.

Gwen looked at the arched portal that now shimmered in the air, a gateway even larger than the *Song*. But the ship would not be sailing through.

Rolling his carpet out on the deck, Sharif sat on it and motioned to Tiaret and Gwen to join him. Meanwhile, Vic and Lyssandra climbed onto a pedal glider that stood near the main mast of the ship. Muscular sailors hoisted the glider up the mast by a rope on a pulley until Lyssandra and Vic were at the very top.

Lyssandra gave the signal. She and Vic began pedaling, and he released the cinches that held the rope. The glider sailed forward toward the crystal door and the new world beyond it. Gwen felt a familiar excitement as Sharif had the carpet take off and fly up to meet the glider in the air.

Together they set off for the marvelous flying city.

CHAPTER 6

I mmediately on the other side of the crystal door, the ocean vanished and was replaced by a sea of undulating sand dunes. Elantya's waves were divided from the desert below Irrakesh only by the glittering veil of the door.

But the pale blue sky above the dunes was dominated by a huge floating island metropolis. Irrakesh was spectacular, even from a distance. Gawking at the amazing flying city and all its unbelievable sights, Vic almost forgot to pedal the glider.

Lyssandra panted and furiously pumped her legs. "You must keep the propellers turning, Viccus, or we will fall."

He snapped his mouth shut so quickly that his teeth clicked together. He looked down and saw only clouds and the desolate landscape far below. "Sheesh, that's a long way to fall." He began to pedal, and their glider picked up speed again, cruising beside Sharif's flying carpet as they approached the fabulous floating city.

To Vic, it looked as if someone had dug Irrakesh out of the ground in one piece with a giant shovel, then flung the whole thing into the air. Now uprooted, Sharif's home city drifted through the skies of this world on a massive chunk of rock.

Irrakesh was a gigantic cluster of buildings and tall towers crowded together on rugged hills, connected by steep streets. The distinctive architecture used stone, tile, and brick, ornamented by friezes, roof crenellations, watchtowers, colonnaded balconies, and pointed ogee arches. Multihued fabric awnings and pennants splashed their vivid colors against the tan and white stone, and long bright ribbons flew from the pointed spires, fluttering in the high breezes.

At the heart of the drifting island, Vic could see the sultan's palace, an imposing edifice surmounted by a large sapphire dome and decorated with small gilded onion domes. Tall, thin minarets at the corners of the elaborate central structure made Vic think of rockets ready to launch.

All along the streets, winding up the hills, a jumble of homes and business buildings piled on top of each other. A labyrinthine section of the lower town held a vast marketplace that reminded Vic of an enormous flea market. A hodgepodge of merchant booths and tents crammed against each other—metalsmiths, woodworkers, potters, fortune-tellers, weavers, spice sellers, and food vendors. Each separate stall was covered with a brightly dyed awning. In talking about his city, Sharif had explained that different colors and patterns of the awnings signified different trades. The streets were crowded with all sorts of people in different clothing that ranged from bright robes to dusty loincloths.

Lyssandra noticed Vic staring. "That is the great bazaar of Irrakesh. I have never been here, but I have seen illustrations. It is quite famous."

"Looks pretty crowded," Vic said. "Sheesh, there must be ten thousand people getting groceries all at the same time."

"Irrakesh has a substantial population," the copper-haired girl said.

Colorful moths as wide as Vic's outspread arms fluttered around the building tops like small children at play. Although he was far above the ground, Vic could hear the everyday noises of Irrakesh's people.

Vic caught a whiff of spices and perfumed smoke as they swooped in lower toward a central gathering square. His stomach grumbled. He always liked to try different things. He saw robed and bearded men standing over what seemed to be cauldrons, waving their hands and summoning up curling plumes of lavender or blue smoke. "Reminds me of a chemistry lab I once had."

Lyssandra shook her head, still pedaling to keep their glider moving along. "Those are viziers. Irrakesh is known for its magic users, very similar to our sages, but they can work slightly different magic, *air magic*. That would help us to defend Elantya."

"I won't forget why we came here. But I could sure use a rest soon."

The flying carpet came close to them, with Piri's glowing orb easily keeping pace, bobbing along in the air. Vic and Lyssandra had to swerve in their much clumsier contraption. Sitting comfortably next to Gwen and Tiaret on his purple rug, Sharif shouted, his face filled with delight. "Is it not beautiful? My city of Irrakesh is the grandest city ever built."

"It sure isn't like anything I've ever seen, I'll grant you that," Vic shouted back, panting. "Are we going to land soon? Some of us aren't on a magic carpet, you know."

At the base of a rocky hill with steep, curving streets that led up to the enormous colorful palace, Sharif descended and found an open square. "We could fly directly to one of the palace balconies, but I would like to show you around first." The pride was plain in the prince's face as he landed.

"Sure, I'll play tourist," Vic said.

"Did not the sultan demand your presence immediately?" Tiaret asked.

Sharif's face darkened. "Who knows what my father will demand of me once he knows we are here? We will see him soon enough."

Sharif carefully rolled up his embroidered purple rug, aligning the edges and making certain that the tassels did not get tangled. On Elantya, he was the only person who had a flying carpet, but they seemed rare even here on the floating city of Irrakesh, presumably owned only by the highest class of nobles.

Their group attracted quite a crowd. Some of the merchants came out to see the cause of all the fuss. Children poked their heads out of second- and third-story windows. A murmur went up from the crowd. "Prince Ali! Prince Ali el Sharif has come back to us."

Blushing, Sharif drew a breath, lifted his chin, and held up his hands. "Yes, I have returned to Irrakesh, but I also have responsibilities in Elantya. There is still much to do there."

Piri bobbed along beside him, glowing a colorful pale blue. She caused as much of a stir as the prince did. "The nymph djinni has grown. See how changed she is?"

"Piri has been through a hard time," Sharif said, "but she is stronger. And I am stronger. I have come to see my people and to see my father."

Vic thought the other boy was showing off a bit. Before becoming close friends with him, Vic had thought Sharif somewhat conceited, full of his own importance. Now, though, he knew that the young man had never wanted to be the leader of

Irrakesh. However, since Azric had killed his brother Hashim, the prince didn't have much choice but to take on the role.

With his flying carpet tucked under the billowing sleeve of one arm, Sharif strolled forward leading his friends. Some of the people cheered him, others simply stared. At one booth, Sharif stopped to examine a rack of long, thick walking sticks made from polished wood tipped with iron. Selecting one, he handed a coin to the seller, who thanked Prince Ali profusely. Sharif then gave the stick to Tiaret and said, "Use this while we are here in Irrakesh. You can take it with you into the palace. It is not a weapon—though I believe you could use it as such, if the occasion arose."

Tiaret nodded her thanks, hefted the staff, and tapped it once on the cobblestones. It gave a pleasing thump, and the girl from Afirik smiled and looked far more at ease.

"Kinda reminds me of Little John's quarterstaff in Robin Hood," Vic said with a grin.

"Was this quarterstaff used for defense, or to assist a feeble person in walking?" Tiaret asked.

"Definitely defense," Gwen assured her.

Vic chuckled. "Little John was anything but feeble."

"Excellent. Then this is my quarterstaff," Tiaret said.

They walked past the tent of a food vendor whose colored awning was electric green and vibrant pink, bright enough to make Vic's eyes ache. But what really caught his attention were the delicious smells. His stomach growled loudly.

Sharif laughed, seeing the hungry looks in his friends' faces, and he went to the vendor. "Are these the best skewers in the city?" he demanded.

"Indeed, they are, my prince." The man puffed his chest with pride. "I guarantee it on my mother's life."

"And is your mother still alive?"

The man hesitated. "They are nonetheless the best skewers in the city."

Sharif chuckled, generously handing over coins. "We will have to see about that." He passed the sticks of savory-smelling meat to Vic, Gwen, Tiaret, and Lyssandra, and they each sampled a bite of the tender flesh.

Vic guessed it was some kind of bird, maybe pigeon or chicken. "It's the best skewer I've ever had in Irrakesh."

The vendor slapped his chest. "You see? My customers are satisfied." The man raised his voice and shouted, "Best skewers in the city! Even Prince Ali el Sharif eats my food."

Pleased, Sharif led them onward, up the steep hill toward the palace. "My world was mostly desert, with many lush oases. Many of our people were nomads, and caravans plied the sands carrying goods from tribe to tribe. At the intersection of these trade routes stood Irrakesh, the one great city, with paved streets and tall buildings, minarets and domes. Long ago, the founders built it near the salt mines and irrigated fields and thick palm forests. But countless generations ago, Azric put a curse on Irrakesh. Our water wells and aqueducts went dry. The air filled with dust. Oases shriveled and turned brown. There was no water for anyone. Our people would have died, had the Air Spirits of Irrakesh not helped our viziers to work a powerful and complex magic. The spell uprooted my entire city, down to its foundations, and lifted it high off the ground, complete with its minarets and spires, domes and arches, palace and bazaars. Since then, Irrakesh has drifted across the open skies, riding the desert winds. Borne aloft, we glide far above the arid, trackless dunes and harvest our water directly from the clouds."

Vic was panting by the time they climbed the last one hundred steps that led to the sultan's palace. "I think the air is too thin up here."

"What *is* the sky but air and water?" Sharif asked.

Vic thought of a few answers, but he didn't have the breath to argue.

In front of the palace entrance, a keyhole arch was tiled with ornate enameled pieces and crusted with large gems. Guards stood outside, holding tall spears whose jagged tips were made of bronze and surrounded by bright feathers. The guards wore gold-scaled armor over their chests and around their waists. Each captain had a tall, crested helmet and a bright purple cape.

The men snapped to attention, straightened their spears. The foremost soldier, with a square-cut black beard, raised his voice and announced, "Prince Ali el Sharif has returned."

"I have come to see my father," Sharif said, striding between the guards. "And these are my friends."

Vic walked close to Lyssandra, and both of them stared wide-eyed at the vaulted main chamber, a place designed to accommodate huge crowds when the sultan himself stepped forward to make pronouncements. At the moment, the palace seemed empty except for a few court functionaries. Several bright green and ruby moths fluttered through open windows and drifted up to the high dome overhead. The bright sunlight cast a sapphire glow as it filtered through the translucent gemlike vault overhead.

Piri flitted ahead, lighting the way. Runners had gone across the vaulted chamber into the many other halls and rooms of the palace. Curtains stirred, and hangings drifted in the breeze. Vic couldn't stop looking around. His neck ached.

Finally, a man glided out, radiating an aura of calm competence that Vic found reassuring. Neither short nor tall, dark nor light, young nor old, handsome nor ugly, the otherwise plain man had glossy golden hair, and his long beard was plaited into a thick braid. He wore a cream turban, and his lightweight enchanter's robes were streaked with the colors of sunset: sky blue, lavender, peach, and rose.

Sharif grinned. "Vizier!" He turned to his friends. "This is Vizier Jabir, my father's most respected and knowledgeable wizard. We will discuss Elantya's needs with him."

"First I must tell you of your father's needs," Jabir said in a reproving tone.

Sharif walked forward. "Yes, my father summoned me, and we came as quickly as we could. He said it was important."

The vizier nodded somberly. "There is little time. We may have a month, certainly no more, and we have much to do. Hurry."

"Much to do for what?" Gwen asked but received no answer.

Sharif's expression did not seem troubled as they all hurried in the old wizard's wake. When Jabir's robe swirled behind him, its pastel colors had a dizzying effect. The vizier pushed thick hangings aside, working his way through one row of curtains after another. Vic felt as if he were struggling through a crowded dress shop as it was getting ready for a sale. He wrestled the cloth out of his way, trying to clear a path forward.

Sharif explained, "These hangings are more than just decorative. They provide a colorful defense against assassins."

"They cannot protect against all assassins, unfortunately," Jabir said as they finally emerged into the sultan's bedchamber.

Sharif's father lay stretched out on an enormous bed surrounded by plump silk cushions, all of them tasseled and embroidered. Tapestries and open-weave mesh hung around the bed. Sharif stopped, staring in disbelief at the sticklike figure amongst all of the pillows.

The old man looked shriveled and drained. He lifted his head and blinked his eyes, at first not even recognizing his own son. The vizier leaned closer to Sharif. "Your father the sultan is dying, and you must take his place to save Irrakesh."

CHAPTER 7

S uddenly Sharif's composure fell away, and in his
reaction to the news, Gwen could see a lonely vulnera-
bility. She wanted to reach out and put an arm around
him to show her support. They had all come along on this
mission to convince Sharif's father that the prince could do
more good for his people by staying in Elantya. None of them
had guessed, however, that the sultan was so close to death.

"What has happened? Who did this to him?" Sharif
demanded. He went to the bed and flung aside the thin hangings with such vehemence that he knocked the rings loose. With
a sound like a sigh, the cloth crumpled onto the embroidered
crimson carpet that covered the tiled floor beneath the bed. Piri
floated behind the prince, glowing a sad dull blue.

Tiaret thumped the end of her quarterstaff on the floor. "Is
there danger here?"

Lyssandra said, "He looks sick. Why would you think anyone
did this to him on purpose?"

"He was so healthy when last I saw him," Sharif insisted,
then lowered his voice. "It has been too long."

The sultan stirred on the bed. His eyes were at first blurry and distant, but then like a candle being lit, they grew bright. Gwen could see similarities between the father and son. Though the old man's eyes were sunken, they were still dark and evenly set below arched eyebrows. His face was thin, emphasizing high cheekbones and a cleft chin.

The sultan drew a deep breath and struggled to push himself into a sitting position with birdlike elbows. He swung a heavy head and his gaze locked with Sharif's. "Ah, my son ... but not Hashim. You are my son Ali. At least *you* have come." He heaved a great sigh, drew another breath, and then struggled into a straighter sitting position. With a surprisingly strong voice, the sultan barked at his vizier. "Jabir, you should have given me notice. I did not wish for them to see me like this."

The old wizard shook his head sternly. "They must know, Sultan."

"They do not need to know everything all at once. Sharif will have enough to deal with."

"These are my friends," Sharif said. "I brought them with me to Irrakesh."

"You no longer need friends," the sultan said. "You need advisors." Then he began a long succession of coughs accompanied by a rattle in his throat.

"But ... what happened to him?" Gwen whispered. She could think of all sorts of sudden illnesses, debilitating diseases.

The vizier said plainly, "Poison. An assassin got past our testers."

"We caught the assassin," the sultan coughed, sounding angered at the thought of the man. "But it was too late. The poison was already inside me."

"Poison." Tiaret looked around, on her guard. "Has the prisoner been interrogated?"

"Yes, and executed," Jabir said.

"But why would anyone want to kill your father?" Vic said.

From his bed, the sultan let out a dry chuckle. "I do not have time enough left to live to explain all the reasons. Imagine hundreds of different factions and families, all of whom have their own needs and desires."

"Our flying city has been plagued by more and more frequent attacks by leathery demons called the terodax," the vizier explained when the sultan could not summon the strength to continue. "The bat-winged creatures were once primitive predators but are now advanced enough to build aeries. They want to attack and kill everyone on Irrakesh and take our city as a great floating nest for their own kind. There is no reasoning with the terodax."

"And one of these things poisoned the sultan?" Gwen asked, trying to follow the story.

The vizier shook his head. The sultan leaned forward on the bed. "No, it is because I sent messages to the aeglors, hoping to form an alliance to protect Irrakesh. Their leader King Raathun said that—for a price—the aeglors would help defend our skies."

Gwen looked from the sultan to the vizier to Sharif. "Are they from this world? And what are aeglors?"

"Both terodax and aeglors share this world with Irrakesh," Sharif said. "The aeglors look human, but with large feathered wings on their backs. They are also more barbaric than our culture here, though we have much more in common with the aeglors than we do with the terodax, who are not at all human."

"Okay, let me get this straight," Gwen said. "First, these terodax are preying on the city, right? Second, you're asking the eagle-winged people to help you protect Irrakesh. Third, someone poisoned you because of that?"

The vizier tugged on his braided beard. "There is a long-standing feud between the aeglors and Irrakesh. No love is lost between us and the eagle-winged men. Many of our noble families resent the very idea of striking a bargain with them."

"Sheesh. Security first, pride later, I say. If it saves Irrakesh, who cares?" Vic asked. "Can't they agree to fight a common enemy?"

"It is a matter of honor. In Irrakesh, blood runs hot when dignity is not properly addressed."

Jabir continued to explain, "The sultan is in constant danger, so we use wards and spells to identify any poison in his food or drink."

"Sounds like you needed to do a better job," Vic muttered.

"The assassin did not use a poison that could be detected. The sultan consumed an inert powder during an extravagant banquet, after which the assassin worked a catalyst spell to convert the innocuous substance into a powerful venom. The sultan would have died that night, so potent was the deadly chemical, but once the toxin was activated, I detected it and concocted an antidote—"

"Then why is my father not cured?" Sharif demanded.

"Alas, Prince Ali, the antidote is but temporary. It can only neutralize the venom for a short time. Poison has sunk its claws into your father's system. It cannot be removed. Each day he must consume more of the antidote just to function."

"Just to stay alive." From his bed, the old sultan coughed. "The assassin belonged to a noble family, many of whose sons had been killed in previous skirmishes with the aeglors. They would rather see Irrakesh crash to the surface in utter destruction than forgive the aeglors."

"That's ridiculous," Gwen said. "They sound like fanatics."

"They are deeply offended. Their priorities are not comprehensible to outsiders."

"They are not comprehensible to me," Sharif snapped, "and I am not an outsider."

47

Jabir shook his head. "No, you cannot afford to be, Prince. You must be one of us now, completely. The people of Irrakesh do not yet know that the sultan is poisoned. We cannot afford panic or dismay. When he consumes the antidote, he is strong enough to perform his court functions ... for a time. You must be crowned before the people can fear that they will be left without a sultan."

Before the young prince could argue, loud bells rang outside. Men shouted from atop the tallest towers and minarets. Others banged gongs. The streets became a flurry of activity and Gwen rushed to the open balcony of the sultan's bedchamber.

Vic hurried to her side. "What now, Doc? Are we under attack?"

"Sounds like an alarm to me," she said.

In the crowded streets below, the people were pulling out awnings, uncovering cisterns. Families and children rushed about, setting out broad pans in the streets. The food vendors and merchants worked to tie down the fabrics of their awnings, covering their wares, their grills. Tiaret and Lyssandra joined them, but Sharif barely seemed to notice the commotion. "It is just a cloud. We are about to go into a cloud."

The bright blue sky suddenly became clumped with dark cottony mist. Irrakesh drifted toward a billowing cumulonimbus mass, and soon the city was wreathed in grayish fog. As they traveled deeper into the cloud, flashes of lightning appeared all around them.

Then the downpour began. Sheets of sudden rain dumped out of the cloud, washing the paved streets, running down in gutters, filling up cisterns and pans and pots, everything the families had set out.

"That is how we gather our water," Sharif said.

The dusty streets quickly became clean. Children ran about laughing in the rain, their loose clothes drenched. Droplets blew back from the balcony, spraying the loosely hung curtains. Gwen drew a deep breath of the fresh-smelling air. She could hear the staccato pattering of heavy raindrops across all the tiled roofs, splashing in puddles in the streets, running in rivulets from statues and pointed turrets.

In only a few minutes, as swiftly as it had begun, the rain stopped, fading away into thick fog. Then Irrakesh burst out of the cloud and into dazzling warm sunlight. Within moments, steam began to curl up from the fresh water on the streets. Brilliant sunlight reflected from stained-glass windows. There was a lull in the conversation and background noise outside, but the activity gradually picked up as vendors reopened their stalls. People emerged from doorways and shelters to continue their business.

Gwen found it amazing, but the people of Irrakesh took it entirely in stride.

The sultan coughed again, demanding Sharif's attention. "I do not have long, perhaps as much as a month, perhaps less. You are my only son now, Ali. My beloved Hashim is dead. Murdered by Azric … but you survived."

Piri flitted in the air, flashing between an agitated orange and the electric green of worry.

To Gwen, the sultan's words sounded like an accusation, as if Sharif had greatly disappointed his father by not dying in his brother's stead. "Therefore, I need to rely on you. We must prepare you for your vital role. There is no more time for dalliances on Elantya, or praktiks in subjects that have no bearing on ruling Irrakesh. Your whole life now belongs to our city. That is why you were born."

Sharif stiffened, struggling to find an argument. "That is why *Hashim* was born. I never expected—" The old sultan's face turned ruddy with anger, but before his father could shout at him, the young man raised his hand. "I know, I know, Father. Do not upset yourself." He sounded deeply sad. "We came here to ask for help for Elantya, but now I must suddenly become an expert in statecraft and court bureaucracy."

"We'll help," Gwen said.

Lyssandra, Tiaret, and Vic all stood close to the young man at the old sultan's bedside.

"Don't worry. We'll all do what we can," Vic said.

"You will do what you must," said the sultan, then he collapsed back on his pillows.

CHAPTER 8

Even after the sultan's shocking news, Gwen could not help but be fascinated by everything around her as the vizier led the five apprentices down palace halls, through a slender, arched doorway in a narrow turret, and up a spiral staircase that seemed to go on forever.

"What is with these people and their stairs?" Vic muttered behind her.

Sharif, who was just ahead of Gwen, seemed to be accustomed to the climb, while Piri danced above his head, twinkling turquoise with excitement. "These towers were built by my people in honor of the Air Spirits," Sharif said. At this, Piri flashed white with pride.

Gwen, who was familiar with her friend's moods and could hear in his voice that he was troubled, asked, "Didn't you tell us you had turned your back on the Air Spirits?"

Hearing the comment, Jabir shot a sharp look back at the friends, and Piri's light dimmed to the dull green of uncertainty. By the djinni's light, Gwen could see Sharif's face flush with chagrin or perhaps guilt.

"For the most part," he admitted. "But not entirely."

"Despite Sharif's misgivings, Piri seems excited to be in the tower of the Air Spirits," Tiaret observed from the rear of the group.

Lyssandra, who was between Vic and Tiaret, said, "That is because Piri is herself an Air Spirit."

Vic sputtered. "She's *what?*"

Gwen stopped abruptly on the stair above him, which made him bump into her. She looked from Lyssandra to Sharif to Piri, and back at Sharif again. "Piri's an Air Spirit, and you never told us?"

The nymph djinni's orb flickered a color dangerously close to red. Avoiding all of their eyes for the moment, Sharif reached down and took Gwen's hand and started back up the stairs again. "She is not an Air Spirit. Not quite yet."

His friends, who were already out of breath from the climb, did not ask him more questions until they all emerged at the top of the minaret onto a balcony that circled the entire tower. The outermost portion of the balcony was protected by a balustrade and gold-wire netting that ran from the stone railing up to meet the edge of the copper roof that sheltered the balcony. Large potted plants with bright flowers filled the open space, and unseen creatures stirred the fleshy leaves.

"What do you mean Piri isn't one of them yet?" Gwen could barely talk as she heaved in long, deep breaths of fresh air.

"He means," the vizier answered for Sharif, "that she has not yet matured entirely ... though she is close." From one of the potted plants, Jabir picked up something that looked like a plump, furry brown snake and stroked it. Gwen stepped forward to pet its glossy furred back as Jabir continued, "Piri is no more one of the Air Spirits—or djinni, as they are sometimes called—than this minkworm is a carrier moth." At this, he lifted one hand and a trio of the brightly colored giant moths that the apprentices had seen when they flew over the city landed on the vizier's arm. Gwen glanced around the balcony and noticed for the first time that dozens of the beautiful, brilliant moths were perched everywhere inside the mesh-enclosed area of the high tower.

"That's a *caterpillar?*" Vic asked, stepping forward to get a closer look at the minkworm. "It's as long as my forearm."

Lyssandra, placing a hand on his wrist to draw the thought from his mind, said, "Yes, it is very similar to a caterpillar, though carrier moths in Irrakesh have much greater intelligence than most moths."

"This minkworm will become a carrier moth." The vizier gave a whistling chirp, and moths flew down to perch on each of the apprentices' shoulders. "The moths are very clever," he said. "They deliver messages and small items around the city much as skrits and aquits do in Elantya."

"Cool." Vic touched a jewel-toned wing of the moth that sat on his left shoulder.

"Piri does not resemble a minkworm," Tiaret observed. "We were discussing Air Spirits."

Jabir agreed. "Her eggsphere is closer to a cocoon or chrysalis in which she will transform into an Air Spirit." He looked more closely at the orb-encased sprite. "She has changed greatly, matured far more quickly than she should have in the past year."

"It was the lavaja," Sharif said. "The accursed Orpheon threw her into the lavaja cracks as a punishment to me."

"But she survived," Gwen said, squeezing Sharif's hand when she saw his flash of sorrow. By the anxiety on his face, she could tell he was not troubled only by this memory, but worried about his father, as well.

Tiaret tapped her quarterstaff on the stone floor. "Piri grew stronger and wiser from her ordeal, as we all did in our captivity."

Again, the vizier nodded. "This explains much. Please sit." He indicated the stone bench that ringed the tower. The moths fluttered away as the five apprentices sat and gazed out through the mesh across the vast and beautiful city. Remaining standing, Jabir studied them in silence for a time, stroking his braided golden beard. Several moths settled on his sleeves, shoulders, and head, but he ignored them. Finally, his eyebrows twitched upward in surprise and his mouth formed a silent O.

"I did not realize. I am in the presence of more than just a reluctant prince, four children, and a nymph djinni." He bowed —not just to Sharif, but to all of them. "The prophecies speak of this. You are the Ring of Might."

The apprentices exchanged surprised glances.

"Viccus and Gwenya are the children of the prophecy—a very important Elantyan prophecy," Lyssandra began.

Tiaret said, "We require Sharif to assist us in defending all worlds. He is part of the Ring."

"I do not wish to disappoint my father or my people," Sharif said, "but each of us here has a special power that we must learn in order to defend every endangered world—not just this one."

Soon they were all talking at once, explaining the Elantyan prophecies, Azric's plan to release his armies, the special bond among the apprentices, and how they had all recently been forged into a single Ring of Might.

"I am not simply a Key to the door of Irrakesh and a prince-in-waiting," Sharif concluded. "I have a new obligation. And I cannot protect my people unless I protect all people."

"I understand," Jabir said, while he wrote a hasty message on a scrap of silken paper. "You have both a responsibility and a higher duty. The demands on all of you are great." He gave the message to an obedient moth, which carried it up to the corner of the filigree net, and Jabir released it to the open sky. "I carry a heavy burden, as well." His lips twitched into a wry smile. "I, too, am more than just Key to the crystal door of this world. Neither am I a simple vizier. I hold both power and influence as the Grand Vizier of Irrakesh."

"In other words, he's their Ven Sage," Gwen whispered to Vic. "Like Rubicas."

"I am also a *Master* Key. I can open the door to any world that is not sealed. And as our people say, 'The blessing of a gift comes not from possessing it, but from using it to benefit others.' I remember all too well how Azric used *his* gifts—to deceive and murder, to gain power, and to change his shape to escape punishment. Thus does evil betray its true nature. I serve the sultan and my people, and if the five of you must defend *all* people to preserve this city, it is my duty to help you however I can."

Sharif sat up straighter, looking less troubled than Gwen had seen him since he'd learned of his father's illness. "It would be most helpful if you could assist us in learning more about our abilities."

"In that case, I believe it would be wisest to do some research in the Grand Library. We must do it today, for tomorrow the prince and I shall stand at the sultan's side while he holds court and signs a treaty with the aeglors."

"Then we will go to the library," Sharif said. To his friends, he added, "The Grand Library of Irrakesh is renowned throughout the worlds."

"I bet it's not greater than the Cogitarium in Elantya," Vic said a bit defensively.

"It is not a competition," Lyssandra pointed out.

The vizier tugged his braided beard. "Indeed not. The library here may not be greater, but it is far different. In fact, young lady," he said with a nod toward Tiaret. "I believe you will be interested to learn that we keep a copy of the Great Epic from Afirik that is current at all times."

Tiaret smiled with genuine delight. "In that case, I believe I have some chapters to add."

With a swirl of his multicolored robe, Jabir said, "Come with me," and led them back down the tower stairs.

Constructed from smooth ivory stone in the shape of a twenty-pointed starburst, the Grand Library of Irrakesh had long arched galleries radiating from a domed central hub. Each branching gallery terminated in a colonnaded veranda. The library floors were inlaid with crystals and marble arranged in complex geometric patterns that, according to Jabir, indicated the subject of the information stored in that area.

The Grand Library of Irrakesh was a technological marvel, filled with books and scrolls, all arranged according to a precise numeric system and stored on shelf after shelf that rotated in an intricate system of noiseless gears and pulleys that could bring any bookshelf down to eye level depending on which text was needed. Unlike the Cogitarium, in this library there was no need for skrits to deliver scrolls. Carrier moths fluttered in the central crystalline dome, enjoying the bright sunlight.

After hours of research beside a beautiful mosaic-tiled fountain filled with cool drinking water, the vizier called a halt to the intense studying. "I believe we now know what we must. All of my reading indicates that your individual skills will be revealed through conscious or unconscious action before they are needed.

"In fact, many of you may have already exhibited your skills without realizing it."

"Meaning?" Vic said.

Tiaret tapped her quarterstaff on her leather-clad foot so as to avoid making noise in the library and said, "I am already aware of my skill. I learned on the way here that I can immediately shut a crystal door at will."

The vizier looked impressed. "That could be quite a useful defense against enemies invading from another world."

"But the rest of us don't really know what our gifts are," Vic said.

As the cousins described how they had come to be in Elantya and what they had done since arriving, the vizier became excited. "So although Sage Pierce is a Key, he did not send you through the original sealed crystal door that led from Earth to Elantya?"

"Our mothers broke the seal on the door years ago," Gwen said.

Vic added, "And Dad followed us through the original door to Elantya just recently. But no, that's not the one we came through."

"Then I believe," Jabir said, "that one of you has a power that no sage or vizier has possessed in five thousand years: creating a new crystal door where none existed before."

"Oh, but we didn't create it. Uncle Cap set up crystals and made calculations," Gwen said.

"Right," Vic agreed, waving his hands like a magician. "If one of us had that kind of skill, then all we'd have to do is kind of think hard about it and hey—Open, Sesame—the door would appear. We know that—" Vic's jaw dropped. For there, behind the trickling fountain, a giant crystalline arch had appeared, glittering like a kaleidoscope of pastel glass shards. And through that arch flew a heavy spear. It passed over their heads and harmlessly struck a wall. Several arrows whizzed through the archway and with reflexes born of their special *zy'oah* training, Gwen and Vic ducked out of the way.

A pair of warriors with raised spears and axes charged through the arch and surveyed the chamber with greedy eyes. Then, with shouts and beckoning motions, they stepped back through, as if planning to bring others with them.

Tiaret jumped to her feet, quarterstaff upraised, and the arch disappeared. "I closed it," she said unnecessarily.

"What *was* that place?" Lyssandra asked, her eyes wide. "They were saying something like, 'Come quickly.'"

"Did you create that door, Taz?" Gwen asked. "It wasn't me."

Vic thought back to what had happened. "I … it wasn't conscious. I was just saying how it would have to work—and it just did."

Gwen shuddered. "Well, I sure hope you learn to control it better than that. It's a lucky thing Tiaret was here."

"I believe our gifts are meant to be used together," the warrior girl said.

"All the more reason not to split up our Key Ring," Vic pointed out.

"I believe the prince will find a way to discharge his duties—all of them," the vizier said. "Just as the rest of you will very soon learn your gifts."

"Um, maybe gifts later, food now." Vic's stomach rumbled. "Suddenly I'm starved."

Tiaret nodded. "I am quite hungry, as well."

"Huh!" Vic said. "Who knew that using magic—even unconsciously—could take so much out of you?"

CHAPTER 9

On the day of the scheduled diplomatic meeting with King Raathun and the aeglors, the city of Irrakesh floated across the skies and stopped over a densely forested valley. Unlike the area from which Irrakesh had been uprooted, Azric had not cursed this part of the world. The enormous floating city drifted lower, controlled somehow by viziers working their air magic.

Vic rushed from one balcony to another, looking down. For two days they had wandered across the empty sky, looking down at a cracked brown desert and a few dry lake beds. During the night, though, they had arrived at an entirely different terrain.

As Irrakesh settled into its new location in the sky, dropping close to the treetops, Vic looked down to see that the forest was not composed of normal trees. Rather than stiff and sturdy trunks, the trees rose on thick, fleshy ribbons of blue-green vegetation held aloft by lighter-than-air bladders, natural helium balloons that lifted the heavy growths high into the sky where flat, ribbonlike leaves spread out to form a canopy.

Vic was reminded of a waving kelp forest under the water, the thick doolya weed that had given them an underwater hiding place when he and his friends were running from the merlons. He saw rounded structures built into the leaves and the thick, fleshy stalks—wooden houses that looked like makeshift nests.

Sharif came to Vic's side out in the warm open air; sapphire blue pennants flapped in the breeze above the balcony. Piri bobbed faithfully along beside him.

"Friend Viccus, the court tailor has provided new clothes for you. We are about to meet representatives of the aeglors, and I would be honored if you would wear princely garb. Gwenya, Tiaretya, and Lyssandra are already dressing themselves in appropriate raiment."

Vic picked up a billowing shirt of shimmering aquamarine fabric. "Hey, this is almost the color of my eyes."

"That was intentional, Viccus."

Vic held up puffy pantaloons, pointed shoes, and a gold sash. "I'm going to look like Ali Baba."

"You will look like a noble prince," Sharif corrected. "Was this Ali Baba a great prince in your world?"

"No … he was a thief."

Sharif snorted. "Then let us hope you look more distinguished than Ali Baba."

After the young man left, Vic dressed as best he could, but the awkward fittings were confusing to him. Two servants fussed over him, adjusting the folds of light green cloth, cinching the sash a bit tighter, then shaking their heads in disappointment. Apparently, he had put the pointed shoes on the wrong feet—something to do with the pattern of embroidery on the side, he was given to understand—but even when he switched them, he couldn't tell any difference. Nevertheless, the servants pronounced him ready....

As Irrakesh cast a great shadow down upon the ribbony canopy of the kelptree forest, Vic noticed a flurry of activity, people moving about, sprinting along the supple leaves and branches. They seemed to be carrying something large and curved on their backs. Then a dozen of the strange-looking men bounced on the flexible leaves and jumped upward, using them like diving boards on a swimming pool. The dark things on their backs were not packs, but revealed themselves to be large, brown-feathered wings! Like great condors, they flapped together and winged up into the sky.

Gwen rushed to the balcony. "Taz, did you see it? Do you see them down there?"

"They must be the aeglors. They remind me of barbarian angels." Then he did a double take as he glanced at his cousin. "Wow. What happened to you?"

"Just a minor wardrobe change," she said, turning in a slow pirouette. Her head was draped with beautiful scarves that were violet like her eyes. Golden bangles dangled from her sleeves and wrists and waist.

"You look like a princess from the Arabian nights. Even better than that I-Dream-of-Jeannie outfit you wore for Guise Night."

"Don't you dare make any cracks about belly dancing," Gwen said, although he knew she had always wanted to try it. He and his father had often gone with Gwen to a local Moroccan restaurant, where they sat on cushions on the floor, ate exotic food with their fingers, and watched beautiful belly dancers perform. Gwen punched his shoulder. "You look like Ali Baba yourself."

He sniffed and lifted his chin. "I do not. Ali Baba was a thief, and I have it on the best authority that *I* look like a prince."

Hundreds of aeglors flew up from their forest city, past the rugged and rocky underbelly of Irrakesh, diving and soaring in the sky. Their wingspans were very wide. Shirtless and very well-muscled, all of the men carried clubs and swords at their waists.

"The aeglors do look like good fighters," he said. "I'd rather have them on our side than attacking us."

"The question is, what are the terodax like?" Gwen said.

In the sky above, he heard loud, shrill cries, like the screams of vultures, but he realized it was the aeglors singing some kind of noble battle cry. With a flurry of heavy wings, they all descended toward the palace. Hundreds of aeglors circled, then settled down onto the numerous balconies and rooftops like a flock of crows. One bare-chested and thick-bearded man was larger than the others; his wingspan was truly majestic. Just from appearances, Vic suspected that this was probably Raathun, their leader.

Gongs sounded. Bugles blasted notes from the tall towers of Irrakesh. Tiaret and Lyssandra came into Vic's room, calling for him and Gwen. "We are summoned to the sultan's main court. Sharif wants us there for the diplomatic ceremony."

Vic took one last glance down at the ribbony, floating forest of blue-green kelptrees where the aeglors made their homes, then he looked up at his friends and was momentarily stunned. Although he couldn't remember ever seeing Tiaret in anything other than her animal skins, today she wore crimson scarves tucked into her waistband all around, so that the scarves formed a kind of filmy skirt. Another scarf fastened to her shoulder straps rippled behind her like a gauzy superhero's cape.

Lyssandra was dressed in a sheer outfit similar to Gwen's, but in a rich emerald green. The diaphanous material flowed with her every movement.

"You, uh ..." He cleared his throat and started again. "You all look amazing."

Lyssandra blushed. "Would you do us the honor of escorting us to the throne room?"

"You bet!" Vic grinned. "I wouldn't want to miss this for anything."

CHAPTER 10

His father's throne room was just as Sharif remembered it, and today the sultan demanded that his only surviving son stand at his right hand beside Jabir. The only weapon in the chamber was the sultan's heavy, curved ceremonial sword, leaning against the back of the throne.

Looking out across the courtiers and the audience in the great chamber, Sharif felt tired and apprehensive. Earlier, he had tried to present his case to his father in private. Not only had the sultan brushed aside Sharif's explanation of the Key Ring, Azric's plan to invade the worlds, and his son's need to assist Elantya, the dying man had insisted on taking a higher-than-usual dose of the preservative medicine that kept the poison at bay in his body. Although the ruler wanted to appear healthy as he signed his treaty with the aeglors, Sharif's father betrayed his anxiety by constantly fidgeting with the jewel-encrusted flute he kept tucked into the sash at his waist. Before Hashim's death, the sultan had often played the flute for his children.

Sharif felt uncomfortable, too, because today he wore princely garb of the finest silks in cream and purple and red and gold. Instead of having his friends beside him, he stood on display for all to see while Vic, Gwen, Tiaret, and Lyssandra, who had just entered looking out of breath, watched from the back of the room. Piri had almost been banished from the throne room as an unnecessary distraction, but Sharif had put his foot down and his father had finally agreed to let the nymph djinni hover hidden behind the prince's back.

Just then, a commotion went up at the back of the room as half a dozen aeglors entered the chamber and, with wings spread wide, marched six abreast toward the throne. Sharif was shocked to see that the largest, most majestic of the aeglors carried a short sword in a sheath at his side. People scattered out of the way, and the aeglors strode up the stairs onto the dais. From the corner of his eye, Sharif could see Tiaret raise the "walking stick" he had given her as she prepared to defend her friend if necessary. Because his people had not trusted the aeglors as long as he could remember, Sharif found he was not averse to being prepared. He was grateful to know his friends were here if trouble should arise.

The most magnificent of the aeglors stepped forward and, at a quick movement of the leader's head, the other five perched themselves on the steps of the dais. "I am King Raathun. I speak for all aeglors," he said. "In token of your sincerity, what do you offer?"

Giving Raathun a regal nod, the sultan motioned for two burly guards to carry a chest forward and set it in front of the winged king, who opened it to reveal gold and bright gems.

"I, King Raathun, accept your treaty on behalf of my people," the aeglor said loudly, so that his words reverberated like a loud screech throughout the chamber.

The sound set Sharif's nerves on edge, but he forced himself to relax and look friendly. The terms of the agreement had been negotiated and approved ... before the sultan had been poisoned.

Raathun plucked a single brown feather from his own wing. "In token of our sincerity, I offer you this treasure."

The leader of the aeglors bent his head toward the sultan and secured the feather with the brooch on the sultan's turban. The two spoke in low tones that Sharif could not overhear. After several minutes of this, the pair pressed their seals to a document that Jabir reluctantly brought forward. Then the sultan stood from his throne and, clasping hands with the king of the aeglors, the two raised their hands overhead.

"My people, we no longer have anything to fear from the aeglors. They are our friends. They will help defend us in times of need, and we will help them, as well."

With a proud nod, King Raathun released the sultan's hand. Motioning to his men to follow, King Raathun walked down the steps of the dais. Together, wings spread once more, they swept from the room.

The sultan turned toward Sharif with a confident look. "You see, my son? *That* is how it is done."

For the rest of the morning, one by one, peasants and nobles were allowed to walk the purple-and-gold carpet that led up the center of the room toward the throne dais and present their concerns to the sultan who, after conferring in each case with Jabir and Sharif, meted out judgment, wisdom, and mercy. Although the prince would far rather have been in Elantya preparing for battle against Azric and Barak and the merlons, he could not help but be moved by the plight of an olive vendor whose entire shop had been destroyed when a brawl broke out in the neighboring booth of a wine merchant. The vizier suggested that each of the apprehended brawlers be put to work rebuilding the olive merchant's shop, paying for the materials out of their own pockets. Sharif advised that the wine merchant feed the olive vendor's family until his business was running smoothly again, and that the two men share the wine merchant's stall equally in the meantime.

In the end, the sultan took both of their advice and also decreed that the brawlers not be allowed one drop of wine until their work was complete. Sharif was amused by the consternation on the men's and women's faces as they thanked the sultan for his good judgment. Piri's voice twinkled in Sharif's mind as she said, *Builders hurry. Finish fast.*

The prince nodded to himself. That had been a nice touch of his father's, with one stroke ensuring that the brawlers would cause no more damage while subtly offering an incentive for them to finish their work quickly. Next, a nobleman approached, and Sharif found himself disgusted with the man's demand that the sultan give him the youngest daughter of a widowed carpet-weaver to pay off a debt that her late husband had owed.

"You cannot allow it," Sharif whispered to his father. "This is barbaric." He could feel Gwen's eyes boring into him from the back of the room, as if accusing his people of being slave merchants.

Jabir, however, gave a small smile. "Perhaps the prince's objections could be addressed if Your Majesty, through your great insight, were to specify the terms of the arrangement."

The sultan nodded with satisfaction. He and his vizier understood one another well. He turned his stern old eyes toward the nobleman, the weaver, and her daughter. Sharif gave a small gasp at what his father said next. "Your complaints have not fallen upon uncaring ears, Lord Iqbal. As complete payment for the weaver's debt, I hereby grant you custody not only of the daughter, Aini, but of the mother."

Sharif felt himself flushing with anger at this injustice, but Piri's gentle voice said, *Wait. More.*

"And as custodian of these two gems of Irrakesh," the sultan continued, "you will feed them, house them, clothe them, and see to even their smallest needs." He held up his hand to stop the nobleman, who was about to object. "Until such time as you find husbands who will make each of them happy, you may not lay one hand on either blossom, unless—by proving yourself worthy—you happen to win her love.

"If you find a suitable match for one of these jewels, bring the couple to me. I will grant my blessing, and you will henceforth be absolved of your duty toward them. But if I should hear of either of these flowers coming to any harm while in your care, half of your fortune will be forfeit to my treasury, and I will use it to feed widows and orphans wherever the need is greatest in Irrakesh." To Sharif's glee the blood drained entirely from Lord Iqbal's face as the sultan concluded, "You will assure me that Aini and her mother are flourishing, by sending them here to my audience chamber every month to deliver reports of your kindness."

"I—I accept your wisdom with gratitude, Exalted Majesty," Lord Iqbal stammered. He reached out a hand to help the widow up from her kneeling position, but quickly snatched his hand back as he remembered the sultan's instructions. The widow gave a bow of thanks to the sultan, stood, and she and Aini walked proudly from the room with the downcast nobleman.

How Sharif wished he could allow himself to laugh at the greedy lord's discomfiture, but he held the laughter in until a teardrop of merriment was forced from the corner of his eye to roll down his cheek. At the back of the room, he saw Vic and Gwen practically dancing with delight as the widow and her daughter passed them.

Trust father, Piri said softly in his mind. *Wise man. Loves people.*

CHAPTER 11

Later that day, the sultan sent Jabir out on his embroidered crimson flying carpet to show off Prince Ali to the people of the city. When Sharif invited his friends along, neither his father nor the vizier objected, and so Gwen found herself sitting once again on a comfortable flying carpet, though the sultan's carpet was much larger than Sharif's and had enough room to seat six adults, as long as speed was not an issue. Delighted with the outing, Piri bobbed above Sharif's head, occasionally flitting this way or that to get a better view of the city below.

"The point of this flight," Jabir explained, "is to encourage the people of Irrakesh after the recent depredations of the terodax." Although they did not know it yet, they were also about to lose their sultan, and the stern but benevolent ruler hoped to reacquaint his people with Prince Ali.

To signal the celebratory nature of their flight, Sharif had dressed in a red brocade vest and pants, accented by a gold silk sash and turban. His arms were bare, revealing the vivid scar of the merlon brand. Jabir gave Vic a silver kite to fly from the back of the carpet; it was shaped like a bird of prey, with multicolored translucent streamers dangling from its tail. Gwen, Tiaret, and Lyssandra each held a cluster of long, bright ribbons tied to a handle that they could wave while allowing the ribbons to trail behind the magic carpet.

"Sheesh," Vic told Gwen, "You look like a high school cheerleader with a mutant pom-pom that grew twenty feet while you weren't looking."

Gwen punched him in the arm with her free hand. "I prefer to think of it as a magic wand attached to a rainbow," she said. She swirled the tip of the wand handle in a figure eight and watched the brilliant strips of cloth loop and flutter like the ribbon of a rhythmic gymnast. "Admit it, Taz—you're secretly jealous."

"No, I'm fine with what I've got," said Vic, pulling on the kite string so that the streamers flowed in a sort of sine wave behind it.

Tiaret, who had tied her ribbons to her quarterstaff, raised the staff high and let the ribbons trail above the carpet like a triumphal banner, while Lyssandra seemed content just to watch her ribbons drift on the breezes. Jabir took the carpet in a dip toward the crowds gathering in the streets below. He made a clicking, whistling sound and moments later an honor guard of vividly hued carrier moths flew beside them.

Prince Ali el Sharif, sitting at the front of the carpet with Jabir, waved down at the people, who cheered and waved back. A broad copper pot sat between Jabir and Sharif. "You may begin now, Prince."

Sharif thrust his hand into the pot and pulled out a fistful of something that he began throwing down into the crowd. Children scrambled to catch them with shrieks of delight. "Candies," Sharif said when Gwen asked him what he was throwing.

Gwen said, "This is just like the Fourth of July parades we used to go to back at home."

"Exactly," Vic said, "only we didn't have a real wizard or a prince. Or flying carpets or floating cities, come to think of it. Other than that, exactly like."

The vizier spoke an incantation and suddenly each of the carrier moths held a mesh bag filled with flower petals. As the moths flew, breezes blew through the mesh of the bags, freeing flower petals, which fluttered and drifted down onto the crowds below. Not to be outdone, Piri, hovering over Sharif's head, let loose a veritable fireworks show of strobes and flashes and sparkles in colors Gwen could have sworn she had never seen before.

As the carpet flew onward, larger crowds gathered in the streets below. Sharif threw more candy to the waiting children. And so it went for nearly an hour—ribbons streaming, flower petals drifting downward, Sharif waving and throwing candy, and Jabir piloting the carpet and replenishing the candy or flower petals with incantations as needed.

The city below was magical to Gwen. To her it was Disney World, Neverland, and stories of the Arabian Nights all rolled into one, but her cousin was not as entranced as she was. When he heaved a heavy sigh, Lyssandra leaned toward him and said, "Is something wrong, Viccus?"

Vic shrugged. "I was just thinking about my dad and my mom and wondering if Dad and the anemonites or Ven Rubicas have managed to help her. We just got Mom back and then we had to leave."

"Our mission to Irrakesh was manyfold," Tiaret reminded him. "We seek help for your mother and for Sharif and all of Elantya."

"I know," Vic said. "I just wish I could see them, that's all."

Gwen knew what he meant. She wished she could see her

aunt and uncle and Rubicas's lab and find out how things were going in Elantya. She blinked, trying to picture them. "It's kind of strange, but now that you mention it, I almost feel like I can see them right in front of us in the air there." It *was* strange. The vision was so real to her that it almost didn't register when her friends started gasping around her.

"You mean like that?" Vic said, pointing to an area just behind Sharif and Jabir where a translucent image of Dr. Pierce bending over the tank holding his ice-imprisoned wife appeared. No sounds accompanied the image.

The vizier glanced back and nodded. "Which of you opened the window?"

"Well, Vic wished he could see his parents, and then I wished it, and all of a sudden, there they were," Gwen said.

Sharif looked back at the "window" and turned to wave at the crowd again. "Viccus has already demonstrated that he can create doors to worlds where no door existed before. I believe you opened the window, Gwenya."

"You opened a window once before," Lyssandra mused. "On top of Ven Rubicas's laboratory."

"But that was with crystals and spells. I didn't know what I was doing," Gwen said. "I still don't."

The vizier said, "True. But you should soon learn how to control your new ability. I believe that before the Ring of Might was forged, none of you could come into your full power. The window and the door you cousins opened were merely reflexive activations by your unconscious minds, under specific magical circumstances. I doubt you could have reproduced the results even if you'd tried."

"Can you do it again now?" Vic asked Gwen. "Close the window and open it again. And turn up the sound while you're at it."

Lyssandra looked at him with surprise. "Can you not hear your father?" Vic shook his head.

"I, too, hear nothing," Tiaret said. Gwen could see Uncle Cap's lips moving in the image, but she couldn't make out what he was saying.

"Sage Pierce is telling his wife that he loves her and that he will continue searching the Cogitarium for any information about ice coral preservation spells. He assures her that, except when he is doing research, he will not leave her side until he can awaken her."

Without turning to look at them, Sharif said, "Lyssandra can hear what none of us can. Is that another gift?"

"I believe so," the vizier answered. "She is a window listener."

When she saw her uncle lower his head to his hands and begin to weep, Gwen quickly closed the window. She opened another window, this one on Sage Rubicas, and found him dozing in his chair over a draft of his shield spell. While Sharif continued his duties of greeting the people, Vic asked Gwen to open a window to let him see his friend Jordan from Stephen Hawking High in California. She did, only to find him walking out of the cafeteria and into the boys' room. She quickly shut that window as well. These windows could be quite intrusive!

"Jordan's taller," Vic said. "Don't you think he's gotten taller?"

"May I see my parents?" Lyssandra asked, so Gwen opened up a window on Groxas and Kaisa. The two stood in the kitchen of Lyssandra's home, their arms wrapped tightly around each other, whispering into one another's ears. Lyssandra's mouth fell open and she blushed furiously. "Close it," she said, putting her hands over her ears.

"Perhaps your gifts are best used only in emergencies," Tiaret suggested to Gwen and Lyssandra.

"You are right," Lyssandra said. "These powerful skills are not to be used lightly."

"At least we know what our gifts are now," Gwen said, feeling relieved.

Sharif threw a handful of candy into the crowd again. "Except for mine."

CHAPTER 12

T he storm clouds gathered in the night sky as Irrakesh drifted along. The thick, dark masses blocked out the stars, filling the open air and even masking the moon so that the light left only a silvery edge outlining the scalloped edges of the puffy thunderclouds. A silver lining … Sharif tried to take heart from that. But his heart was heavy from the bad news Piri had broken during the banquet.

Before the feast, the sultan had consumed another dose of the antidote to the poison so he could function well enough through the busy activity. Although the court functionaries, other noble families, and minor viziers saw nothing wrong in his performance, Sharif recognized the tremor in the old man's hands and the grayish cast to his skin. In spite of his worry, Sharif had forced himself to eat normally. Then Piri had blindsided him, explaining in her short bursts of words what would happen. He had already lost so much … and tonight he would lose another very important part of his life.

Now his spacious bedchambers seemed to echo with loneliness. Inside her transparent shell, Piri hovered in front of him. He could see her small doll-like form placing her hands against the curved boundary as if trying to get out. Her long hair floated about her small, perfectly shaped head as if static electricity filled the egg. The colors shifted, but kept returning to the deep purple of love.

Too sad. She waved her hands, looking at him. *Don't be.*

"I can accept it, Piri," he said, "but that does not mean I can be happy about it. I am even a little frightened. As my people say, 'The sadness after a loss is a measure of what one had.' And I had so very much, Piri."

Gwen and Vic, Tiaret, and Lyssandra stood at the entrance to his bedchambers, calling out to him.

"Is now a good time?" Gwen asked.

"You said something about teaching us court games," Vic said, "but I'm guessing you just wanted to talk."

Sharif drew a deep breath to gather strength and turned to face his friends. "No, neither talk nor games, Viccus. I simply needed you here with me."

Gwen came in, her expression sad and concerned. Piri floated over Sharif's shoulder, and he took great comfort just from seeing the nymph djinni. With his four friends there with him, and Piri, his new bedchamber no longer felt so echoingly empty. The gigantic suite not far from his father's palatial chambers had seemed far too extravagant—too much room, too many colorful fabric hangings, too many pieces of ornate art. The walls were intricate mosaics. Each covering on his bed competed with the others for intricacy of weaving and embroidery. The vaulted ceiling overhead, with its patterned tiles and gold edgings, seemed to swallow up every sound. He felt as if he could be lost here.

When he was younger, these quarters had seemed perfectly ordinary, his due as the second son of the sultan. But he had spent the last year in students' quarters in Elantya, and in a fairly small chamber working with Sage Rubicas. He had forgotten how to be ostentatious. The sheer size of his rooms no longer represented wealth or grandeur for him, but the weight of his responsibility.

At first Piri had flitted around the room, raising her lighted sphere all the way to the high ceiling and shining down like a miniature sun. Now, though, she appeared much more somber. He knew he should be happy for the nymph djinni, but he was secretly relieved that she seemed as affected and uneasy as he was.

Gwen and Vic went to stand out on the balcony, looking up into the backlit clouds.

Tiaret, however, picked up on the prince's apprehension. "You seem unsettled, Sharif. Is something unpleasant about to occur?"

Lyssandra's large cobalt eyes were filled with worry. "I do not understand it, but I had an uneasy dream last night. In an older dream, I saw Azric, huge and towering in the clouds. This seemed something like that … only different."

Before Sharif could summon the courage to answer, Gwen pointed upward. "It looks like a thunderstorm. I think I saw lightning."

"That is not lightning," Sharif said, then swallowed hard. "It is the Air Spirits. It is the djinni."

They all gathered on the balcony, where the wind had begun to whip coolly around their faces. Sharif took a deep breath and smelled the dampness. Flashes of lights appeared in the clouds like the sky fireworks Lyssandra's father created in Elantya. Piri bobbed in the air, glowing brighter, flashing. Sharif thought perhaps she was signaling into the sky.

Sharif concentrated on his story. Talking about dry facts and history eased the lump in his throat. "The djinni are powerful beings who have helped Irrakesh in the past. The adults become Air Spirits and live in the clouds. They can project images of themselves vast enough to frighten anyone. Although I know they are our friends, even I find them intimidating."

"I thought genies were supposed to live in bottles or lamps," Vic said. "That's how it is in all the stories I've read."

"This isn't a story, Taz," Gwen said, giving him one of her get-a-grip looks. "It's real."

"Right," he said with a hint of sarcasm. "Come on, Doc. We're on the balcony of a sultan's palace in a giant flying city looking into the clouds for Air Spirits, and we took a flying carpet ride to get here. Sheesh, all we need now is some computer graphics or Ray Harryhausen to add the special effects."

Sharif pressed on, though his eyes kept drifting to Piri. "Djinnis have their own powerful magic, a life energy that they can expend to create things that most people would consider miracles. Someone ambitious and power hungry can find ways to trap a djinni, to enslave it and force it to do that person's bidding. But the djinni are clever as well as powerful, and very often when a person utters such a wish, the captive djinni will twist the command, making the wish turn out unlike what the master expected.

"A person with selfish wishes can usually only hold a djinni for no more than three wishes. After that, the djinni is able to break free."

"See? Genies and bottles and three wishes," Vic said. "Just like in the stories."

"Long, long ago, when Azric came to this world for the first time as a powerful dark sage, he captured and imprisoned several Air Spirits. Each wish drains part of the life force of the djinni who grants it. Azric used his wishes to wreak great destruction and added his dark magic to dry up and shrivel much of the landscape. Millions of people and djinnis were destroyed. Irrakesh would have died as a city, but many of our citizens sacrificed their lives to free the djinni and foil Azric's plans. As a reward, the Air Spirits became our allies. They expended some of their powers to help our viziers uproot Irrakesh, so that it could rise above the devastation and fly forever. Since that time, the people of Irrakesh have sworn never to make demands or wishes of the djinni. That is why they continue to help us. That is why they trust us." He reached out his hand, spreading his fingers, and Piri drifted close to it so that he could lovingly caress her sphere.

"An excellent story," Tiaret murmured.

"Why do you have a nymph djinni, then?" Gwen asked. "You never told us how you actually received Piri."

"After the shape-shifter Azric murdered my brother Hashim, I was angry with the Air Spirits. Their magic is sufficient to detect a dark sage, yet they did not. They could have warned us —should have protected Hashim from him. Their sorrow for our loss was great, and the Air Spirits tried to comfort my family, but I would hear none of it. I turned my back on the Air Spirits and vowed neither to help or rely upon them again.

"Nymph djinnis are slow to mature and are very rare. When my father brought me Piri, I did not stop to think of the honor the Air Spirits did us by trusting me with their only nymph in a century. I accepted her as a valuable trinket which, in my arrogance, I believed I deserved. But I cared for her, and she soon became my closest friend. I understand now that the Air Spirits let me have her for a time to comfort me and to reestablish trust with my family. I did not, however, deserve her."

In the clouds, the lights grew brighter, flashes of lightning flaring like molten gold, spilling through the swollen cumulus. The clouds themselves seemed to be reshaped. Piri throbbed yellow-white, lifting herself high in the air above Sharif's head.

In a hoarse voice, the future leader of Irrakesh said, "A nymph djinni should not reach maturity for many decades, even a century. I believed Piri would be with me for all of my life. But when Orpheon threw her into the lavaja cracks, the power there changed her, accelerated her. Piri matured much sooner than anyone expected. Tonight she will shed her shell and become a free djinni."

His voice cracked. "Tonight she must leave me."

Piri leaned down inside her sphere. *Must go.*

Sharif turned to Gwen, struggling to retain his composure, trying to keep his voice steady while tears burned his eyes. "Tonight she joins the other Air Spirits. Piri is still very young, and once she sheds her shell, she will be extremely vulnerable to capture. I could not risk her. Only other djinnis can hope to protect her."

Waves of emotion swelled within him, and he couldn't speak for a moment. How unfair it seemed. He was not ready for this. Not only had his father called him away from student life in Elantya, changed his future, and increased his responsibilities, but even more had changed. His father was dying, and Sharif was powerless to help him. Sadly, Sharif would become sultan far sooner than he had expected, and on top of that, he would have to do it without Piri. It felt like too much, this abrupt and painful lesson in growing up.

The swollen clouds had grown much closer. With flashes of lightning, faces began to form, huge, towering shapes, a handsome but stern-looking bald man with a pointed beard and long curled eyebrows. There was a beautiful woman, too, her projected hair tied into a topknot. Her smile was sincere, her eyes as bright as dazzling fires. Her refined features reminded Sharif of Piri's tiny face. He could see what his own nymph djinni would look like when she grew up.

Sharif heard shouts and calls from other balconies and

towers throughout Irrakesh. Many people had noticed the strange visages. A nymph djinni was rare even on Irrakesh, and when one returned to the Air Spirits, it should have been cause for great celebration. But the sultan was too ill, and Sharif felt too sad to stand among the crowds. He did not know how he could tolerate the cheering of so many people while waving farewell to his beloved Piri. He wished he could do this in private, with no one but his closest friends.

Piri seemed to grow larger, and her sphere became misty as it spread out, expanding. As the faces came closer, lightning bolts arced across the clouds. "Piri, our daughter. We have come for you. Return with us to your destiny," the giant male face boomed in a voice louder than thunder.

"We will take you home with us to the skies, child," said the mother.

Behind those faces in the clouds appeared numerous additional projected heads, a shimmering chorus of other djinni. Sharif raised both hands. Gwen and Vic gasped. Tiaret stared, clearly impressed by the sheer power the djinni projected.

Lyssandra had tears in her wide eyes. "This is what I saw in my dream."

"Go, Piri. Be safe and be strong." Sharif's voice nearly broke.

Now the shell dissolved entirely, and the small doll-like djinni grew larger and at the same time less substantial. Free now, she flew away, streaking across the sky. Piri circled the great towers of Irrakesh, dipping low over the sapphire dome of the main palace, rising up to the tops of the tallest pointed minarets. She seemed exhilarated by her freedom, and though Sharif felt tears trickle from the corners of his eyes, he was happy for her. He knew this was where she belonged.

Many of the djinni drew closer, welcoming her. Even Sharif's breath was taken away by the nearness of the enormous Air Spirits. He had been angry with the awesome presences since the death of his brother Hashim. He had said terrible things and turned his back on them. Now, though, he knew he had been wrong. It was not for him to dictate what the Air Spirits should do.

Impulsively, Vic began to wave his hands. "Wait! Hey, djinnis. We have a request. We need your help. My mother is frozen in ice coral. Azric captured her."

Gwen shouted out, adding her voice to his, "Yes, you hate Azric, don't you?"

In unison, the glowing, towering faces in the clouds scowled. "The people of Irrakesh do not make demands of the djinni," said the male voice who seemed to be Piri's father.

"We're from Elantya, not Irrakesh," Vic said desperately. "We can—"

Sharif put his hand on his friend's shoulder. "We are not trying to enslave you," Sharif said to the Air Spirits. "Piri can tell you who we are and what we have done. She knows the threat Azric poses. Listen to her. It is our hope that you will help in this great battle."

Piri swooped back down to hover in front of him, absolutely beautiful, wispy and insubstantial, shimmering with light and power. His heart ached. For years he had offhandedly considered her no more than a pet or a possession, but when he'd lost her among the merlons, he had learned to value Piri, understood how close they were.

Depart now, she said. *See family.* Then she smiled, her hair rippling about her face. *Will return.* With a brief backward glance, she glided up into the clouds. The other djinni gathered around her in a joyous reunion. The enormous faces turned back to Irrakesh. Sharif gave them his entire attention, knowing that half of the population of Irrakesh was also watching in awe.

"We will learn of Azric's plans, and we will consider your words," said the male voice.

Then, like a dissipating storm, the Air Spirits, with Piri, faded away into the roiling clouds. Sharif continued to stare, trying to see his friend for every last second, but she was gone. Though he still felt the weight of responsibility on his shoulders, he could not ignore the emptiness in his heart.

CHAPTER 13

B efore dawn, Gwen was deep in a dream about opening crystal windows to look in on her friends from Earth when she was awakened by the vizier. "Lady Gwen," he said in a whisper, "the prince requests your presence."

Her eyes sprang open and, although it was still dark in the drifting city, she was instantly alert. "What's wrong? Is he hurt?" Automatically following the vizier's lead, she kept her voice low as she threw off the silken coverlet on her cloud-soft bed.

"Not hurt," Jabir said. "Merely in need of a friend. His father has taken a turn for the worse." He turned to glide out of the room. "I will wait for you in the corridor."

Having lost both of her own parents, Gwen understood all too well why Sharif would need her support right now. She quickly pulled on a pair of sheer pantaloons and a flowing, gauzy blouse over the brevi-like garment she had worn to sleep in. Careful not to disturb Vic or Lyssandra, whose beds were separated from hers by lightweight silk curtains, Gwen padded barefoot to the door of their chambers where Tiaret stood, walking stick in hand.

"I heard the vizier enter and could not sleep," the other girl explained to Gwen. "I will remain here and keep watch." Overhead, a lazy fan stirred the warm air in the room. "I perceive no immediate danger."

Gwen, feeling reassured to know that her friend was not alarmed by the early morning comings and goings, followed the vizier down several breezy passageways to the sultan's chambers. Inside, past the ornate hangings, Sharif sat at his father's bedside, his face etched with worry. An old serving woman dipped a cloth into a basin of water, wrung it out, and placed it on the sultan's forehead.

The sultan's breathing was labored, and perspiration shone on his skin in the light of the oil lamps that lit the room with their soft glow. Sharif's olive eyes were welcoming and grateful when he looked up at Gwen's arrival. He motioned toward something his father held in his hands: the bejeweled flute she had seen tied to the sultan's sash on several occasions. "He won't let go of it," Sharif murmured. "For some reason, it seems to comfort him, although he does not have the strength to play it."

At this, the sultan roused slightly, waved the ornate flute and pointed to Jabir, who stood just behind them.

"As you wish, Your Majesty." The vizier took a vial from the polished marble table near the sultan's bed and poured a few drops of potion onto the ruler's lips. "There is not much left. In one of their raids, the terodax destroyed the ingredients I had collected for another batch. You have three, perhaps four, doses —enough to last a few weeks at most." Jabir sighed. "Each time, your father waits longer and longer before taking the potion. Twice he has almost died because he did not wish to waste one moment as leader."

The potion seemed to have an almost immediate effect on the dying man. Color seeped back into the sultan's cheeks. His eyes flickered open and focused on Sharif and Jabir.

"Thank you, my friend," the sultan said to the vizier. "I understand that there are limits even to what such a powerful wizard as you can do against this poison." His gaze lowered to Sharif. "Your time to lead may come sooner than expected, my son. You have much left to learn. If only Hashim were still here. He always knew how to comfort me." He shook his head sadly. "You have great responsibility, my son, but for now I must speak in private with my vizier."

Gwen could see the pain on Sharif's face when his father spoke about his murdered son. After she and Sharif waded back through the colorful cloth hangings to the antechamber, Gwen nibbled at the edge of her lower lip and asked a question that had been plaguing her for the past few days. "Are you certain you can trust him? Jabir, I mean. He's not setting off any of my alarm bells, but you said that years ago Azric disguised himself and managed to weasel his way into your father's confidence. How can you be sure that Jabir is trustworthy?"

"He has proved himself often over the past several years. Jabir never set out to find wealth and power. Most of the money the Grand Vizier earns goes toward housing and educating orphans in the poorer parts of the city and ensuring that no one starves to death or lacks for honest work to do." Sharif's expression reflected genuine admiration. "Jabir does not wish the Sultan of Irrakesh to spend one coin less on the people of our city in the mistaken belief that everyone is already looked after. He realizes, as I do, that there is still much to do for our people. As the wise ones say, 'A caring heart sees needs to which the eyes are blind.'"

As if speaking that phrase had been too much for him, Sharif's composure crumbled, and he leaned against Gwen for support. Gwen knew the prince would normally have turned to Piri in such a time of great upheaval, but even that comfort had been taken from him. He pressed his face to her shoulder and mumbled, "I am a prince, so everyone expects me to be mature, to know what to do, to be confident. But I am not ready to rule. My wisdom is no match for Jabir's, and my father longs for comfort that only my brother could give him. For years I have lived with the knowledge that my father would rather I had died than Hashim, and it angered me, for my grief was as great as his —even if he did not realize it. His contempt for me made the situation all the harder. Now I do not know how I can endure the loss of my father."

His voice was so choked with pain that Gwen could not think of a single thing to say to comfort him. When her own parents had died, nothing anyone had said had eased the hurt. Her throat tightened at the memory. Each murmur of, "You'll always have your memories of them," or "Your parents will live on in your heart," or "Time will heal the wounds," had scraped at her already raw feelings.

"Both of my parents died," Gwen murmured. It sounded like a terrible thing to say, but she wanted Sharif to know that she understood the pain, the confusion. She would not insult her friend by offering him easy words of false comfort. But Gwen could be here for him, and she would listen. She put her arm around him.

After a time, Jabir came into the antechamber and said, "His Majesty is exhausted, even after the antidote. He will sleep for several hours now." The vizier withdrew to his own rooms, leaving Sharif and Gwen alone again.

"How will I bear it?" Sharif said in a muffled voice against her shoulder. "First Hashim, then Piri, and now my father. If I cannot face these losses, why would my people ever think me fit to rule Irrakesh?"

"I don't know." Gwen ached for him. "Nothing really prepares you to lose a parent, Sharif. Nothing completely fills the lonely spot they leave in your heart when they die." For years, she had hidden her own heartache beneath a stoic veneer, not showing her emotions or truly sharing her grief with anyone, even Cap and Vic. But here in the antechamber of the sultan's apartments, she came face to face with those feelings again, and suddenly, as if a dam were breaking, tears flooded down her face and her body shook with great, wracking sobs of anguish that she had never fully released since the loss of her parents.

Now, arms wrapped around each other, Gwen and Sharif both wept for the loss of loved ones and the loss of their childhoods. Gwen wept for the jokes her father would never tell her, for the holidays their family would never spend together, for the milestones of life her parents would never be with her to witness. And as she cried, the pain began to ease. Gradually, as sunlight seeped over the horizon, a calm stole over them, the child of the prophecy and the son of the sultan. Their tears dried and they sat together on the silk cushions of the window seat, hand in hand, watching the sun rise.

"You know," Gwen said, breaking the silence, "your father isn't dead yet. If I could have even one last day with my parents, I'd spend it doing everything I could to show them how much I love them."

He closed his eyes for a moment in thought. "I have been cursing my misfortune at having to watch my father die, but perhaps in this I am more fortunate than you." He opened his eyes. "You are right. My father is still alive. I know of something that may lift his spirits—a confection of honey and crushed sesame seeds that he and Hashim loved, and they always agreed that only one merchant made it properly." He stood, pulling her up with him.

Gwen gave him a nod of encouragement. "Then that's where we'll go. Let's bring the others."

The bazaars, or souks, of Irrakesh were noisy and crowded, the small streets winding and confusing, full of merchants hawking their wares. The air was heavy with the tantalizing aromas of baked goods and roasting meats. No matter which direction Vic looked, there was something interesting to see: a snake charmer making a glistening silver serpent sway to his haunting tune, a troupe of acrobats performing amazing feats for anyone who would stop to watch, a painter whose canvas was the skin of any man or woman who wished to be adorned—kind of like a tattoo artist, Vic supposed—a pair of jugglers passing ripe fruit back and forth between them, a band of minstrels playing drums and stringed instruments while a young woman clad in pantaloons and scarves danced and clinked tiny finger cymbals together.

Holding Gwen's hand, Sharif led the way through the cramped cobblestone streets, intent on his mission to buy a gift for his father. But that didn't mean Vic couldn't enjoy himself while they were out. "Now this is my kind of place." Beside him, however, Lyssandra looked troubled. "What's wrong?" he asked. "Don't like the music?"

"Viccus, I … I saw this place. I dreamt it," she said.

Tiaret looked down at her petite friend and gave her quarter-staff a tap on the cobblestones. "The meaning in your dreams is not always plain, but it is often unpleasant. Perhaps we should all remain close together. There may be danger."

The three of them hurried to catch up with Sharif and Gwen, who were now stopped at a booth with a blue-and-yellow striped awning. The woman at the booth was wrapping up a parcel and handing it to Sharif. "Made fresh by my husband just this morning. The best in all of Irrakesh."

Handing her a coin, Sharif thanked her and took the package. "We have one more visit to make," he said, leading them through a narrow alley and up another cobblestone street to a wine merchant's shop. Beside it, several shirtless men were hard at work constructing what looked to Vic like one of the nicest booths he had seen in all of the souks.

"Prince Ali," the wine merchant gasped. "You do my humble shop great honor."

"What can I offer you?" another man said, appearing beside the wine merchant. "Olives? Dates?"

With excitement, he handed out samples to each of the apprentices. They enjoyed these offerings, which Sharif generously paid for. The merchant had just poured them each a cup of cool frothy ale when a loud shriek overhead made Vic drop his on the cobblestones. The friends looked up to see a horde of leathery winged creatures gathering over the city.

"Uh-oh," Vic said. "Looks like some refugees from Jurassic Park just arrived, and they don't look friendly."

The terodax plunged toward the crowded streets.

CHAPTER 14

As the monstrous terodax began their attack on Irrakesh, Tiaret thought they were the most hideous creatures she had ever seen. She had battled the bristling and foul-smelling corpse-hyenas that the sand warriors rode during the Grassland Wars. She had personally slain a swollen vampire snake in the stony foothills beneath the cloud forests. More recently, she had fought the merlons and their fierce captive creatures.

These terodax, though, were different. Like demons, they had long, leathery wings with jagged edges and sharp horns on the points. Their heads, elongated in order to accommodate all the teeth in a narrow but powerful jaw, were covered with inter-locked bony plates that served as tough armor. With eyes as solid black as obsidian marbles, the creatures had long pointed tails that could be used as weapons, in addition to the serrated sword blades they carried in the clawed hands on their well-muscled arms.

They flew together in regimented formations behind a flock leader, demonstrating both organization and intelligence. They cawed and shrieked, using no discernible language. They made a rattling, grinding sound with their weapons across spiny wristlets on each forearm. The very noise hit the high edge of Tiaret's hearing ability, set her bones trembling, and invoked an instinctive fear. But she grasped her quarterstaff, spread her legs for a sturdy stance, bent her knees slightly, and prepared to fight. These things could be killed. That was all she needed to know.

Hundreds upon hundreds of the terodax descended, beating their taut, leathery wings, looking like a greenish-black swarm in the sky. Tiaret was reminded of vultures circling over a fat carcass out on the Veldt. The people in the bazaar ran for shelter. An entire family of vendors ducked through the low doorway of a tan stone house, leaving their pottery and painted tiles unattended.

One of the terodax flew low, slashing with its saw-edged sword, and ripped apart an emerald-green awning over a food merchant's stall. Stumbling backward, the man shouted curses at the enemy. The vendor's brazier tipped over, spilling his skewers of spiced meat to the ground. The fire in the cooking dish caught the tattered awning and flames began to lick upward.

A handful of terodax swooped low, ripping through tents and awnings, knocking down a wooden framework built against the side of a stone tower so that the frame fell apart, leaving only a few scraps dangling from the tower wall.

From the high windows, archers launched a volley of arrows, and four of the brash terodax fighters dropped squawking out of the sky. When the winged creatures struck the streets, two were dead and broken. Other wounded monsters flailed about while angry citizens ran forward with their clubs to batter the enemy until all of the fallen terodax lay bloody and dead on the streets. Angry merchants hurled stones and sharp objects at the attackers above them, but the terodax seemed to taunt them, flapping their wings and easily dodging the projectiles. Now that the people of Irrakesh had begun to fight back, the terodax truly became cruel.

Three more flew in low, as if targeting Tiaret and her friends. Sharif dove under a table just as one of the winged warriors clattered down after him, splintering the surface, knocking glittering bits of beaten metal jewelry all over the street. Vic held up a polished rock that some vendor had been trying to sell as an ornament. He squinted his eyes, concentrated, and hurled the projectile. It struck one of the terodax directly beneath the bony headplate, blinding it. "Whoa—bull's-eye!" he called.

The disoriented terodax reeled dizzily, dipping downward, and as soon as it came within range Tiaret lunged forward and swung her quarterstaff with all her might. The iron tip smashed the opposite side of the creature's head, knocking it unconscious. Still twitching, it crashed to the ground. She did not hesitate as she slammed the staff down again, breaking its skull.

Converging on their true target now, the swarm of terodax dropped lower, their wings flapping with sounds like hollow drumbeats. Gwen ducked, and Vic knocked her the rest of the way to the ground, barely avoiding the attack of the winged creature. The cousins reacted swiftly, using moves they had learned in their intense *zy'oah* training. Tiaret swung with her staff and thrust it so hard into the ribs of the terodax that it punctured the thick hide. The creature flew upward, shrieking, panting, and obviously in pain. A rain of its blood spilled down, and the creature wove drunkenly through the air before finally slumping motionless onto a rooftop. The Irrakesh archers launched more arrows, but they could only pluck the terodax out of the sky a few at a time, and increasing numbers of the winged creatures seemed to swoop in from nowhere.

"This is the largest attack I have ever seen," Sharif cried.

"The terodax normally prey upon a few unsuspecting people at a time, snatch babies or livestock, steal any supplies they can find, and then fly away."

"This is not a skirmish," Tiaret said. "This is a war." One plump, white-bearded merchant who sold lanterns shouted defiantly at the attacking creatures. Two terodax dropped down, selecting him on purpose. Though he tried to scuttle out of the way, one grabbed the fat man by the shoulders, while the other grasped his ankles. Digging their talons into his skin, they flapped their broad wings and lifted him up into the air. He screamed and thrashed, flailing his arms, but he could not break their hold. Tiaret watched, feeling a sickness in the pit of her stomach but knowing she could do nothing. The terodax flew with their captive out beyond the edge of the flying island city— and released him. The lantern seller's screams quickly disappeared into the winds as he fell thousands of feet to the cracked ground below.

"Come. This way," Sharif said, leading them through the winding streets. "I know the nearest armory."

"Shouldn't you get to safety instead?" Gwen said. "First, the odds don't look good here. Second, you're part of the Ring of Might. Third, you're the next sultan, and you can't risk leaving your people leaderless."

"I cannot leave my people to fight without me," Sharif said.

The terodax operated now in a furious concerted attack, snatching up their victims and dropping them off the edge of the city. Tiaret felt a cold fury building as she watched dozens of innocent citizens plunge to their deaths. The terodax dove repeatedly, trying to seize the apprentices, but Tiaret defended them. The five friends ran, letting Sharif guide them through the maze of streets. Lyssandra threw a few objects up at the winged creatures, while the cousins improvised, using *zy'oah* fighting techniques.

"Sheesh, we just barely got the hang of fighting merlons," Vic muttered, grabbing a heavy copper pot and banging a terodax on the head with it.

Sharif led them doggedly onward. Reaching the small, barred armory alcove, Sharif found that the city guards had already been there. "Here. This is all that is left." He took a spear and a dagger for himself and handed out long, bronze-tipped weapons to Gwen, Vic, and Lyssandra. Tiaret declined. She gave her quarterstaff a twirl overhead. "This is sufficient."

With a flurry, the pedal-glider-sized creatures came down, circling over the friends. The terodax slashed with their jagged swords, trying to drive the companions into a dead end in the tangled alleyways. People rushed in all directions.

Gwen and Vic took their spears and jabbed upward in unison, stabbing the thighs and stomachs of two attacking terodax. Another winged creature thrashed with its forked tail, smashing marks into the brick walls of the alley. Lyssandra reacted swiftly, swinging her spear sideways and using the long, sharp-edged blade to chop off the creature's tail. With a shriek that warbled up beyond her range of hearing, the monster flew away, thrashing and bleeding.

"They hope to corner us," Sharif said.

An old woman tried to make her way uphill, seeking shelter. She was exposed in the alley. Tiaret ran toward her, hoping to protect her, since the old woman could not move swiftly. She looked up into the sky, her wrinkled face filled with fear. Then one of the terodax seized her, tangling its foot talons in her shawl and pulling her into the air as if she were no more than a toy. Tiaret could do nothing to help. The terodax flew away over the rooftops, and she knew that the old woman was doomed.

Furious at what she had just seen, Gwen hurled her spear. The long weapon flew true and stuck one of the flying warriors in the back. It flapped and thrashed. Frantic in its efforts to escape, it did not look where it was going, crashed into the side of a tower, and fell to the ground, dead. Seeing the wooden scaffolding up the side of another tall minaret, Tiaret sprinted toward it. She used one hand to pull herself up, scrambling higher and higher until she stood on the rickety platform. Terodax swept toward her, and she swung the quarterstaff like a club, bashing one and then another out of the sky.

As the flying creatures fell stunned, Sharif and her other friends dispatched them before they could do further harm. Tiaret's arms were already sore, muscles aching from the strenuous fight. She tossed her head to clear her vision and shake off the sweat that dripped down her forehead. She could still see countless numbers of the winged enemy coming in waves. This attack seemed to go on and on, and she knew that from where they were, the people of Irrakesh could not defend themselves. Although the city guard continued to launch arrows, killing more of the enemy, their efforts would never be enough.

Suddenly, though, Tiaret heard shrieking whistles, birdlike cries, and a loud brassy tone like bugles. From the other side of the sky, sweeping out of the fuzzy white clouds, came a second winged army. These, however, were much more humanlike. Their broad wings were covered with brown feathers that resembled those of a gigantic eagle. The bugle sounded again.

"It is the aeglors!" Sharif shouted.

Vic whooped, and Gwen started jumping and applauding.

Lyssandra stared with her mouth partially open. "The aeglors have come."

Tiaret twirled her quarterstaff in the air, and the second group of winged beings flew in, a full-fledged airborne army— exactly the alliance the sultan had requested. She swung the quarterstaff, almost offhandedly now, and smashed another opponent. Irrakesh was saved!

CHAPTER 15

The sight of the terodax attacking and killing the good citizens of Irrakesh infuriated Sharif. Whether or not he had wanted the task, he was to be their sultan, their leader.

The broken and bloodied bodies of the winged creatures lay in the steep streets of Irrakesh, many of them studded with arrows, others knocked out of the sky or clubbed down by Tiaret, who still stood like a dervish on the scaffolding, swinging her quarterstaff at any creature that came in range. These monsters had taken a terrible toll on the city.

All across the city, amidst the shrill cries of the horde of terodax, he heard an uproar of cheers from the people, who had seen the aeglors. Sharif now understood the many reasons why his father had been willing to break tradition and form this unprecedented alliance with the eagle-winged people.

Vic straightened, lifted his chin, and grinned as the cloud of aeglors flew forward, ready to crash into the terodax. "This should be good."

In the vanguard of the terodax, Sharif had identified their

leader, the creature with the widest wingspan and the longest curled horns, as well as a scarlet, bony head crest. The leader let out a loud, howling shriek that seemed more like a monster's roar than any sort of language. But the terodax understood the strange warbling words, and they began to pull upward. Sharif could tell they were forming ranks, ready to stand against the oncoming aeglor army.

With a fiery look on his face, Vic hurled his spear at one of the last terodax, whose talons and fangs dripped with the blood of two more helpless merchants. The spear skewered it in the stomach and the terodax fell thrashing and shrieking. Sharif knew that Vic had been appalled when he'd killed a merlon who'd threatened to murder Tiaret under the water. Though the terodax looked even less human than the merlons did, he could see that the young man from Earth was still bothered by so much bloodletting, but he clearly had no choice. So many of the flying creatures were still attacking Irrakesh.

Now that the aeglors were here to drive back the winged predators, he doubted that anyone on Irrakesh—even the most vengeful of the old noble families—would complain about the alliance the sultan had made. He kept his gaze on the bearded and muscular King Raathun, who led the charge, bellowing in his deep voice. Flapping their wings, the aeglors approached the massed terodax like a gathering thunderstorm. With a long, sharp sword in one hand and a spiked club in the other, King Raathun looked like a harbinger of destruction just waiting to be released.

But the titanic clash in the air did not occur.

The aeglors flew in amongst the winged predators without striking a blow, without fighting or snarling, and joined with them into a single much larger flock. The sounds became a raucous cantata of shrieks, caws, bellows, and high-pitched squeals. Then the combined group of flyers dove down to begin a second assault on Irrakesh.

"What is happening?" Lyssandra said.

"We have been betrayed!" Sharif said. He remembered an important saying of Irrakesh, that deeds proved friendship more faithfully than words. King Raathun, who had signed a pact and made promises, now showed his true intentions. The aeglors were in league with the horrific terodax.

A roar of dismay rose and fell among the panicked population of the city. The guards of Irrakesh poked their heads out of the towers, nocked their arrows to their bows, and prepared to make their last stand. They launched volley after volley into the sky.

Fighting side by side, the aeglors and terodax crashed down in an utterly overwhelming force. The enemies of Irrakesh had literally doubled.

Sharif's heart sank. He knew there was no chance whatsoever his people could win. As the battle was engaged, Sharif called to his friends, and they tried to run back to the armory alcove to get more weapons, while Tiaret stood defiant on the scaffolding. Her dark face was set with a determination to fight until the very last moment. Sharif couldn't see how any of them would survive.

But, while the terodax had been like wild dogs attacking anything and anyone, dropping their victims off the edge of the flying city or tearing them apart with their talons, teeth, and saw-edged blades, the aeglors had another plan entirely. King Raathun bellowed orders and his winged soldiers flew in pairs, holding webbed netting between them.

Sharif saw the aeglors winging toward them, holding their nets ready, and suddenly realized their plan. "We must find shelter." He shouted up at the scaffolding, "Tiaret, come down!"

"The fight is unfinished," she said.

"You will be captured. They want us. They want hostages." He turned. Lyssandra was already pulling Vic into a narrow, crowded alley where she didn't think the aeglors could go.

Several terodax dropped to the ground, standing with their wings spread, their clawed hands holding sharp weapons in front of them, blocking the alleys. Sharif turned and tried to pull his friends in another direction, but an aeglor warrior stood in their way. The flying man's eyebrows were thick, bushy, and drawn together, like caterpillars butting heads.

Overhead, Raathun yelled to the leader of the terodax, berating and insulting him. The terodax leader snarled and snapped in response, but Raathun was not impressed.

Aeglor warriors dropped down lower, holding their net.

Sharif pulled out his dagger. "Back-to-back," he said to Gwen. "With me. We cannot let them capture us."

Raathun's voice boomed as he overheard Sharif. "We will capture you. Be thankful I have talked this primitive creature out of killing you outright." The terodax leader hissed and cawed. Raathun snapped, "You are stupid. You cannot plan ahead. There was a far simpler way to end this battle that would have cost far fewer of your people—not that a hundred dead terodax are any great loss."

The scarlet-crowned creature shrieked, and Raathun lashed out, "I should kill you myself for putting these valuable hostages in danger. You do not know how important they are. Azric gave us explicit instructions."

"Azric!" Sharif cried, shocked to hear the name of the dark sage. Even so, the pieces began to fall into place.

Raathun let out a loud, rumbling laugh that made his dark beard quiver. "Yes, Azric. I believe you have met him. And I believe your brother knew him quite well ... especially in the last few moments of his life."

Sharif tried to hurl himself up into the air at the attackers, but the aeglors dropped the long, tangling net over him and Gwen. Another group of the winged men snared Vic and Lyssandra, while two terodax wrested Tiaret's staff from her grasp, plucked her from her high position on the scaffolding, and brought her down, scratched and bleeding from minor wounds, to drop her amongst the other captives.

"Wrap them up and fly them to the palace," Raathun said. "We do not want them wriggling their way free to drop and make a mess on the streets far below. This will be our new city, the flying aerie of the aeglors. It will be difficult enough cleaning the human vermin out of their hiding holes."

Sharif struggled, but the strands of the net bound him too tightly. The threads were made of some kind of elastic contracting substance. He had heard of the fibers the aeglors extracted from their tall and flexible kelptrees. He knew he wouldn't be able to saw through the strands even with his knife.

As the aeglors lifted him up in the air, his stomach lurched. He and Gwen were pressed together in a tangle of arms and legs, looking down through the openings in the mesh to see themselves being carried swiftly over the rooftops. The surviving members of the Irrakesh guard shouted and cursed. A few still launched arrows until their captains ordered them to stop for fear that a stray shaft might kill the prince or one of his companions.

Sharif was so incensed at the betrayal of the aeglors that he could barely spit out his words. "Why are you doing this? What did Azric promise you that goes beyond what the sultan agreed in your alliance? You swore an oath."

"I swore an oath to a *human*," Raathun said. "That means nothing. Azric promised to give us Irrakesh once the humans are removed. Your people should not be in the skies. You are not meant to fly. Irrakesh is offensive to us, and when the aeglors inhabit your towers and your palace, it will become our great fortress in the sky. We will fly far from our forest home. We will command this whole world."

Next to him, the leader of the terodax snarled. Raathun didn't take the creature seriously. "I do not know what Azric promised to these ... things." The terodax leader shrieked in annoyance, but Raathun didn't try to understand.

Gwen squirmed, tipped her head upward, and spoke boldly to the aeglor king. "If you can so easily break your word to humans, what makes you think Azric will keep his promises to you?"

"He must," Raathun said, his voice booming. "He would not betray the aeglors."

"Now we know you have bird brains to go with those wings," Vic scoffed.

"Insult us all you wish," Raathun said with a deep-throated chuckle. "But you are our captives, and we have just conquered Irrakesh. The palace is already secure, and we will soon convince your sultan to surrender the whole city without further fighting."

"My father will never surrender," Sharif snapped.

"We both have confidence in the old sultan," Raathun said, "but we expect different things of him."

Fires from the previous attack had begun to spread through the marketplace as tent cloth, draperies, and awnings burst into flame. Looking down at the disaster, Sharif felt a blade of dread pierce his heart.

They flew over the palace, which now looked like a rookery with so many flying creatures, both terodax and aeglors, circling the highest minarets, clustering on the domes and pointed rooftops. They flew in through the open balconies and sat on the sculptures that embellished the entrances around the sapphire dome. As they flew in through the open keyhole arch that formed the grand entrance to the sultan's throne room,

Sharif saw that five of the palace guards lay bloody and dead on the tiles outside the entrance.

Inside the vaulted throne chamber, hundreds of aeglors and terodax strutted about. Sharif saw some of the winged creatures dragging away dead bodies, some human, some terodax or aeglor. Jabir, in his sunset-colored robes, struggled and thrashed, but he was bound with thick ropes. A gag had been placed in his mouth, so that he could speak no spells.

The old sultan, looking grayish and weak, had been yanked from the throne and pushed forward; Sharif guessed his father was far closer to death than the prince had seen him since returning to Irrakesh. The sultan had expected to spend the day "in contemplation"—which meant resting and conserving his last remaining energy. He had little of the antidote left, and Jabir had said his body could tolerate no more of it.

Unceremoniously, the aeglors dumped their netted captives on the floor. One of them began plucking at the strands binding Vic and Lyssandra. Another winged man released the now-weaponless Tiaret, who sprang to her feet, looking warily around the room but knowing better than to throw away her life in a pointless attack. King Raathun used his long, sharp blade to slice open the net that held Gwen and Sharif. He grabbed the prince roughly by the shoulder and hauled him out. He yanked the young man to his feet and held him threateningly. Ignored, Gwen freed herself from the severed net and stood, looking indignant.

"I have asked for your surrender," Raathun said to the sultan. "You will now send word that all of your guards are to cease fighting. Tell them to throw down their weapons and bow to their new rulers, the aeglors."

"I will not," the sultan said. "I would rather see Irrakesh destroyed." Sharif knew that his father meant it. "I will tell my vizier to reverse the spell that keeps our city flying. Irrakesh will come crashing down."

"You would never do that," Raathun said, his voice rumbling. "And I would be all too happy to kill every one of your humans and throw them over the edge, but for some odd reason Azric does not want that."

The sultan struggled to remain upright, his grayish face turning red with anger. "If Azric ever sets foot here in Irrakesh, I will destroy him."

"Bold promises for such a weak man," Raathun said. "I could have my people and these other ... creatures," he gestured to the terodax with a sneer, "work for days just slaughtering you all, but I am not a patient man. I have waited far too long for Irrakesh." Now he grabbed Sharif by the hair and jerked his head back. He pressed his sharpened sword edge against Sharif's bare throat. "This is your chance, sultan. I know he is your son. Surrender Irrakesh now, or I will behead him while you watch, and then before he stops bleeding and twitching, I will call my aeglors and tell them to massacre your entire population."

Shuddering with the strength of his inner fury, Sharif struggled, but the razor edge of the aeglor's sword pressed into the soft skin near his jugular vein. "Do not do it, Father." His stomach knotted. He couldn't help but remember all the disappointment his father had experienced, all the deprecating things he had said about Sharif's ability to lead, how he could never be a strong leader like his brother Hashim.

Sharif drew a deep breath and waited to die. The old man had never been flexible or compassionate with him. Sharif was sure his father would make the right decision.

Instead, the sultan broke down sobbing. "I cannot endure the death of two sons." His shoulders slumped. "Take your blade away from him." The sultan could not look Sharif in the eyes. "I am sorry."

Raathun let out a loud laugh.

"Father, no!" Sharif snapped. "You cannot. Think of all the—"

But the sultan glared at him and held up a hand in a gesture that abruptly silenced any further words from his son. "I still rule here, and I make the decisions." He looked at Raathun. "Irrakesh is yours."

CHAPTER 16

Things were bad, very bad. Gwen, Vic, and their friends had come to Irrakesh to request allies for the island of Elantya, assistance in healing Kyara, and the temporary loan of the prince of the realm. Instead, Irrakesh had been captured, the Air Spirits had declined to do anything for Vic's mother, and Sharif's father was dying. The people of the city had been disarmed or imprisoned. In addition, all five of the friends were now trapped in the flying city when they should have been hurrying back to Elantya to defend it.

Now that the sultan had surrendered his city, all of the energy seemed to drain out of him. He wavered and collapsed on the polished steps in front of his throne. The jeweled flute came free of his sash and clattered on the floor. Gwen gasped as the sultan's turbaned head hit the tiles with a dull crack. Kneeling beside his father, Sharif picked up the flute and tucked it back into the sultan's sash. The friends all tried to run forward to help, but aeglors held them back. Somehow managing to duck free of their winged captors, Lyssandra bent over the sultan and, removing the stopper from the tiny crystal vial around her neck, dribbled a few drops of restorative green-stepe into his mouth. A bit of color came back to his cheeks, and he seemed to breathe more easily, but Sharif's father did not wake up.

Somehow, Vizier Jabir managed to dislodge the gag that had kept him silent. "The poison is too strong," he said in a voice heavy with sorrow. "The sultan belongs in his bed, not on the floor."

King Raathun motioned to two of his guards, who picked up the sultan unceremoniously by his hands and feet and followed Jabir out of the room. Sharif still knelt on the floor, his head bowed. "My father, the great and wise ruler of Irrakesh, a captive in his own palace."

Though the prince resisted, Lyssandra made him drink some of the restorative brew as well.

"Can this get any worse?" Vic mumbled. "A dying ruler, the city invaded by enemies, the would-be allies turn out to be traitors? Have we run out of clichés yet?"

Just then, the aeglors fluttered their feathered wings, producing a sound like muted applause. They raised their voices in loud shrieks and raised their eyes to something that flew toward them across the city. *A flying carpet?* Gwen wondered. *Another aeglor or one of the prehistoric-looking leathery winged creatures?* But it was even worse.

Beside her, Vic groaned. "I had to ask."

It was, in fact, a terodax flying toward the palace—the largest one Gwen had ever seen—and on its back, his arms spread wide as if to embrace the entire sky realm, sat a man she knew all too well. Breezes whipped the long, straight, black hair away from a youngish face that was handsome but at the same time wrong somehow, even from this distance. Gwen could see the man who had killed her parents: Azric.

The ancient dark sage guided the terodax to land on the

railing of the terrace outside the throne room. Once perched, the creature bowed its head low to touch the tiled floor, and Azric gracefully dismounted, landing nimbly on the floor before the captive apprentices. A mixture of tension, fear, and anger seemed to squeeze all of the breath out of Gwen. Sharif struggled back to his feet, and Tiaret took up a wary defensive stance.

Azric swept his mismatched blue and green eyes around. "Ahhh, all present and accounted for, I see. Well, almost. Tell me, where is the sultan?"

"In his own apartments, ill unto death's doorway," the king of the aeglors said. "He will not last long."

This brought a look of great pleasure to Azric's face. "Excellent." Gwen wanted nothing more than to put as much distance as possible between herself and this evil man, but she and Vic did not dare show weakness. The dark sage had come so close to controlling them when they were captives among the merlons. She and her cousin had to demonstrate immediately that they would unseal no crystal doors for him.

The dark sage folded his hands in front of him, steepled his index fingers, and chuckled with delight. "The city captured, several extra hostages, and the children of the prophecy as a bonus. I can scarcely believe my luck. Only it's not luck, is it? *She* told me it would be so."

Gwen cleared her throat. "Who is 'she'?"

Azric smiled as if this were a brilliant question. "Why, the last of your merry band, of course. Oh, didn't I mention it? I brought your friend with me." And from a satchel hanging at his belt, he took out a kind of carafe with a broad, bulbous base, a long slender neck, and a stopper at the top. The amber and purple glass of the bottle was etched with intricate designs that seemed to glitter from a faint light within it. "Your little, very useful djinni."

"That can't be," Vic began.

"Piri!" Sharif cried with shock.

"Release our friend," Tiaret said in an ominous tone.

"Piri would never help you," Lyssandra said.

"She might," Sharif said with a look of horror. "She would have no choice, once he imprisoned her."

Gwen could hardly believe what he was saying. "Why?"

"Because Azric captured her in that bottle," Vic said.

Azric gave Vic an encouraging nod. "Your little friend, however reluctant she might be, serves *me* now." He made a small moue of disappointment. "Alas, she has not yet come into her full djinni powers. Her magic is not strong enough to grant my wishes. Her abilities to shed light or to float through the air and water are of little use to me, but she was exceedingly easy to capture. Very weak and helpless. And I do have this power over her: I can make her tell me the truth. I ask a question, and she is forced to answer it honestly.

"Naturally, answering questions drains substantial energy from her," he said, shaking the faintly glimmering vase. "Just as granting large wishes would drain the life force from an adult djinni. But Piri has been quite useful to me thus far. I asked her how best to capture Irrakesh, this gem of the skies. She told me the perfect timing—and that the sultan would surrender his city if his son's life hung in the balance." Sharif winced at this revelation.

"Sadly, I learned thousands of years ago that not even the Air Spirits are capable of unsealing a crystal door." Azric gave a wistful sigh. "Imagine my disappointment. Still, it was amusing to watch that one djinni try. Unsealing a door was the only request I made of it, and the Air Spirit tried and tried until it used up its entire life force and disappeared into nothing." He grinned at the apprentices as if he had just shared a charming joke with them. Then, ignoring their angry glares he blithely continued, "In any case, I knew that capturing Irrakesh and destroying Elantya were only preliminary steps to my ultimate goal."

"Releasing your immortal armies?" Gwen asked sharply.

"And conquering all known worlds?" Vic added.

Azric placed his spread hands palm to palm and tapped his fingertips together. "Naturally. And for that, I still needed a *seal breaker*, as the legends foretold. So imagine my joy when I asked Piri how to get my hands on you, and the poor thing told me that both of you were already here in Irrakesh, ready to be presented to me, like roast ducklings on a platter. And so, once I dispose of Elantya, the three of us will have all the time we need to break the seals without a single meddling sage to get in our way. You could save us all some trouble and agree to help me now, Vic and Gwen." He raised his eyebrows. "There is no hope of defying me."

"There's always hope," Vic said.

Azric brushed this aside. "Now that my victory is almost at hand—with the help of King Barak and his merlons, along with my flying allies—I've been thinking again about my ancient armies." He gave a casual shrug. "Which general is the strongest, which army to free first, how best to contact them, and so on. You know, the usual." Azric offered them a thin smile.

"So I asked Piri if there was a way to look in on my armies. I know they are still alive, of course, but I haven't seen them in thousands of years." He stopped tapping his fingers and rubbed his hands lightly together. "And guess what she told me?" His odd, unpleasant eyes bored into Gwen's. "Our dear Gwen has a skill that I had not even imagined. As much as I have enjoyed the anticipation, I see no need to wait any longer. Gwen, I will tell you the name of a world I wish to see, and you will show it to me. Let's start with Ga'arbyl, shall we?"

Gwen blanched and swallowed hard. "I don't know if I can just show you a place I've never seen." She waved a dismissive hand, but the words died in her throat as a bright, flat picture automatically appeared in the air between her and the dark sage. The edges were misty and blurred to soft focus, but the center was sharp and clear. In the silent image, thousands upon thousands of armored soldiers were gathered in what appeared to be the courtyard of a massive castle. A lavish feast was laid out on long tables set with roasted meats and heaped with fruits and loaves of brown bread. Many of the warriors held flagons of ale or wine.

The image showed a man clad in heavy armor and a blood-red cape. The battle helmet on his head seemed to resemble a crown. He stood on a wooden platform at the center of the revelry. "Excellent—that is Oshilbraq," Azric said.

Gwen found herself fascinated by the spectacle in the soundless window image. Oshilbraq raised his hands high in the air. The silent armies seemed to cheer wildly. Oshilbraq swept an arm to one side and several of his men lifted a struggling soldier onto the stage. This one wore no armor. At a command from the warrior king, the man got to his feet and stood meekly next to him. Gwen's heart froze at what happened next.

The image of the formerly cowering man rippled and changed, his hair growing darker, his skin paler, and his beard seemed to absorb itself into his face. His clothing changed to silken robes, and in moments, an absolutely perfect duplicate of Azric stared out at the crowds. Judging by the dark sage's startled look as he observed, it was clear that even Azric himself had not expected this.

The crowds of soldiers in the courtyard seemed to go wild with excitement, jumping and cheering and waving swords or spears over their heads. Embarrassed at having done Azric's bidding so quickly and so thoroughly, Gwen glanced around at her friends. Sharif was distraught. Vic looked more interested than concerned. Tiaret seemed very suspicious, and Lyssandra looked deeply troubled. Gwen wasn't exactly thrilled about the situation herself.

In the image, enthusiastic soldiers threw garlands of flowers at the Azric doppelganger. The man, apparently getting into the spirit of the event, caught the garlands and hung them around his neck. At this, the crowds became even more frantic until the Azric copy, with a running leap, threw himself from the stage into the crowd. Catching him, the soldiers raised him on their shoulders and carried him through the courtyard past the crowds. The immortal warriors raised their tankards, as if in a toast to him, and drank. Azric, the real one, seemed both pleased and annoyed with this spectacle.

The king aeglor whispered into the dark sage's ear.

"That is enough," Azric said to Gwen. "For now. I'd like to see more. I really would. Though it is unsettling to see someone masquerading as me, it is quite clear that my armies still revere me. But I have worlds to conquer, and I can waste no further time watching such revelries."

CHAPTER 17

I hate heights," Vic groaned, clutching the iron bars of the cage he shared with Sharif and Lyssandra. It squeaked as it rocked in the endless breezes. In some places the bars were so far apart, a thin person might be in danger of falling out.

"That was never one of your phobias before," Gwen said, who sat in an identical cage with the stoic Tiaret. "Remember the time we climbed that high fire lookout in Sequoia National Park?"

"This is different," Vic said, squirming, adjusting his feet, trying to find any comfortable position. Vertigo assailed him. The distant ground spun dizzily beneath him. His foot slipped between the bars and dangled sickeningly through the opening. "I've never been suspended miles above the ground in a giant bingo cage before—or maybe this is Thunderdome. I hope not." Sneaking a wary glance at Sharif, he shook his head. "Two men enter, one man leaves." Lyssandra helped Vic pull his foot back in and balance himself in an ungainly squat.

After being captured by Azric's aeglor-terodax alliance, the five friends had been separated into two of the three spherical cages attached to the rugged, rocky bottom of the flying island that was Irrakesh. The prison-globes were made from thick strips of black wrought iron, but Vic saw distressing signs of rust—or maybe old bloodstains. He couldn't tell.

Each cage hung from iron-link chains bolted to the solid rock overhead. As the flying city drifted along so far above the ground, wind swung and rattled the cages. The third spherical cage held nothing but a weathered skeleton—all that remained of some long-forgotten prisoner who had died up here.

"In generations past, the sultans used this punishment for only their most vile criminals," Sharif said. "It was called the Deepest Dungeon. The villains were hung down here, exposed to the elements."

"It must have been awfully difficult to feed prisoners," Gwen said.

Through the bars of his cage, Sharif peered at her. "No one fed them. It was a permanent punishment. These cages were meant to be so strong a deterrent that there would be nothing left but a few bones before Irrakesh needed to use the Deepest Dungeon again."

"Sheesh," Vic said. "I hope we get paroled before that."

Fortunately for the apprentices, Azric did not want them dead, and the aeglors had no trouble reaching the cages. Winged warriors dropped down below the base of the island and came up from underneath. They gave each prisoner a packet of dry, flavorless food and a small container of water. Ravenous, Vic ate so quickly that he was dismayed when several large crumbs broke off of the tan, crumbly wafers and dropped down to be swept away by the winds below.

Tiaret seemed perfectly comfortable beside Gwen, unbothered by the great gulf beneath them. She slipped her long, muscular legs through the bars and let them dangle. It appeared to be a much more comfortable position than Vic's awkward squat, but he couldn't bring himself to relax. He attempted to open a crystal door inside their cage, but it didn't work. He didn't know why. Maybe he could not create one so small or so close to himself, or maybe he didn't have enough energy.

Gwen, however, was able to do something none of them thought possible. Absently touching the xyridium pendant on its thong around her neck, she wished aloud that she could make a window to find out what was happening in the city above.

"You can't," Vic pointed out. "Irrakesh is in the same world we're in, not through a crystal door. That's not how our powers —" He stopped short as *somehow* windows opened for Gwen outside their cages.

One window showed Azric alone on the throne in the sultan's throne room. In another, Vizier Jabir was being tortured by a handful of aeglors. Gwen shut that window quickly, and Lyssandra did not need to tell anyone what she had heard.

When Gwen opened another window to peek into the sultan's bedchambers, the rooms were empty. At the sight, Sharif made a choking sound and gripped the bars of the cage so tightly that his arms shook with tension.

Vic could tell the effort of opening this "local" window was draining Gwen. She looked as if she might collapse from the strain, and they were all wary of what they might see next. "That's enough for now, Doc. Rest now, spy more later."

She let her hand fall away from the xyridium pendant and the window closed. The friends sat for a long time in silence.

The flying city moved quickly, driven by magic and no doubt guided by Azric now. The aeglors had taken possession of many of the buildings, rousting out the human inhabitants and turning them out into the streets, while the terodax circled Irrakesh like guard dogs. Vic guessed that although the winged men might have preferred to dispose of the humans, Azric would not allow it—not because the dark sage felt any compassion or sympathy for the enslaved populace of Irrakesh, but because he saw people as subjects and workers, and Azric did not waste things that he could use.

Much of the landscape of the world below was monotonous and brown, as if they were in an airplane flying above Death Valley forever and ever. Vic had looked down at the American desert once when he and his father had taken a plane trip north from San Diego just before Gwen had moved in with them.

Soon, however, the monotony changed—for the worse. Vic noticed a foul, sulfurous odor burbling up from cracks in the ground far beneath him. Terodax shrieked and squawked with excitement as the city approached the devastation. Vic thought he heard a low rumbling in the distance below, and he saw black cinder cones, volcanic chimneys that spat out scarlet lava, sending thick plumes of volcanic smoke into the air. Many more terodax flew in the air, circling volcanic mountains, making their nest cities inside the mouths and craters of extinct volcanoes. Active volcanoes erupted, sending rivers of lava oozing across the blasted landscape.

"My eyes feel as if they are on fire," Lyssandra said. Stinging tears streamed down her face.

Vic tried to brush the tears away, but his own eyes were just as red, and he kept blinking. His lungs burned, and the fumes grew more and more difficult to breathe. "This must be what the terodax call home, sweet home," he said.

Their leader, with his scarlet head crest and long horns protruding from the sharp angles of his wings, was accompanied by several other predators, all flying in perfect formation, as if they took every cue from their leader's movements. The creature flapped his wings and hovered in the air, looking as if his desire to rip Vic and the other apprentices into pieces was foiled only by the bars of the cage and his fear of Azric. The leader's pointed tail thrashed as he drifted there.

The terodax leader let out a bone-chilling shriek and a roar. He snapped his fanged jaw shut and jerked his head sideways in a gesture that seemed to signify tearing meat. Interpreting the large creature's intentions as less than friendly, Vic replied with his own nonverbal communication—he stuck out his tongue.

"Don't make him angry, Taz. Are you trying to get us killed?"

"Bravado now, jail-break later," Vic said. "Anyway, what makes you think he knows what it means?"

The terodax let out another whistling yowl and winged away, taking his companions with him. Up above in Irrakesh, Azric was probably making plans and giving King Raathun control of the city. No one knew if Sharif's father was still alive, but the old sultan had been very weak already and was, at the very least, nearly dead from the long-acting poison he had been fighting. Vic didn't know how they were ever going to get out of this. But "hanging around" here until they turned into skeletons was not an option for the Ring of Might. If the prophecies were right— and at this point Vic fervently hoped they were—the fate of entire worlds rested in the hands of the five friends. They *had* to escape.

"Can you not summon the djinni to help us?" Tiaret called to Sharif.

The prince shook his head. "Even if I knew some trick by which to call them, no one can command an Air Spirit unless he holds that djinni captive through evil magic." His brows drew together, and his voice went hoarse. "I believe Piri wishes to help us, but she cannot, for Azric now holds her."

Just then, a dun-colored giant moth fluttered down among the hanging cages. It looked just like the messenger moths that Jabir had kept, but Vic couldn't remember any of them being quite as plain as this one. It almost blended in with the dirt and rock under the city—which perhaps was the point, Vic realized.

Without hesitation, it flew to the cage Sharif, Vic, and Lyssandra were in. The creature had a tiny scroll tied to its leg, and Sharif retrieved it. As soon as the prince held the message in his hand, the dun moth flitted away.

Sharif unrolled the scrap of parchment. "It is from Jabir," he said and read it aloud. "Do not despair, Prince. Your father lives. Azric watches me closely, but as our people say, 'A disciple of hate commands no power to rival the might of love.'"

"That sounds promising, at least," Gwen said. The landscape, however, had no cheer to offer them. Below they saw a field of volcanoes, some belching fumes, others like cauldrons filled with boiling lava, and even more of them dead cinder cones crawling with a huge population of terodax. "Look at all the destruction," she said. "It seems like places where the terodax and the aeglors live are the only parts of the surface that were spared. And even that doesn't look too appealing."

"Didn't Azric ruin most of this world?" Vic asked.

"Yes—with a curse. My world is just a start, however," Sharif said, staring downward at the blasted terrain. "If Azric succeeds in breaking open the sealed crystal doors and unleashing his indestructible armies, all worlds that resist him may end up like this."

"That is possible. But there is something important that I did not tell you about Azric's deathless warriors," Lyssandra said. "The images you saw in the window that Gwenya opened did not tell the entire story."

"True," Tiaret agreed. "The Great Epic would not be complete with pictures alone. Words are necessary to impart understanding."

"Then it is fortunate for us that Azric could not *hear* what the soldiers in the window were saying. Their traditional Festival of

Azric has been held for thousands of years. But they do not celebrate the dark sage. They despise Azric and curse his name."

"Are you sure?" Vic asked her. "Sheesh, they looked pretty happy to me."

"They were," Lyssandra assured him uncomfortably, not meeting his eyes. "I heard many comments that led me to this conclusion. One soldier said that he wished the feast were over already, so that the crowds could begin their revels, torturing and dismembering the false Azric all night."

"Eww," Gwen said. "I'm not sure I really wanted to know that."

Tiaret seemed greatly interested, however. "The man who stood in for Azric—was he an immortal warrior, as well? If so, he could be dismembered, but he would not die."

Lyssandra nodded. "But immortals can still feel pain. Another of the soldiers laughed and said that he longed for the opportunity to chop the real Azric into small pieces, and then— once Azric reassembled himself—rip him to shreds all over again." The interpreter girl shuddered.

Vic said, "Cool."

Astonished by her cousin's apparent insensitivity to suffering, Gwen shot him one of her I-can't-believe-you-just-said-that looks.

"Don't you get it?" Vic said from the other cage. "This means that even if Azric did manage to get through the seal on that crystal door, his armies aren't exactly going to be happy to see him."

"Not in the way that Azric would wish them to be happy," Sharif corrected. "But with their door unsealed, the deathless armies could still conquer many unsuspecting worlds."

"Then we must see that they do not escape," Tiaret said.

"How can we stop them from escaping when we cannot even free ourselves?" Sharif asked.

CHAPTER 18

At night the iron cages still creaked, the sulfurous air still stank, and the lava cracks in the ground below them still glowed like the dying embers of a campfire. Gwen felt they had been hanging there forever.

That day they had watched the terodax flying in regimented patterns after their broad-winged leader. She wondered if the flying creatures had a hive mentality and he was "king bee," or if they were simply a well-coordinated flock following a single point bird. She had seen birds in formation before. Though she wasn't convinced that the monsters had high intelligence, they made up for any lack of brainpower with brute force.

Azric had not come down from the city overhead to taunt them, but Gwen was sure the dark sage would eventually try to force his captives to do his bidding, using the Ring of Might to his advantage. This long silence was not hesitation on Azric's part. Rather, she knew he was softening them up, tormenting them, hoping to weaken the five friends. Well, she vowed, he would be in for a surprise.

In the dead of night when the aeglors had clustered in the

towers of the human-built city above and the terodax had gone back to their nests in the volcanic craters below, Irrakesh drifted in silence, cages dangling beneath it. In the other occupied cage Gwen could see her friends' forms as shadows, lit only by the reddish glow from below.

"Maybe we should try a sing-along," Vic suggested. "A little 'Kum Ba Yah' to keep our minds off our troubles?"

Gwen snorted. "First, singing would call attention to ourselves—the wrong sort of attention. Second, the fumes from the volcanoes are making my throat raw. And ..."—she fumbled for another point—"third, your singing voice is terrible." She knew the criticism wasn't fair, but she was beyond irritable. Breathing volcano vapors had made her feel woozy, and her rear end was numb from sitting on metal bars all day.

Tiaret sat up, apparently not as affected by the day in captivity as her cage-mate. "I could recite portions of the Great Epic. Let us hope that someday our present actions will be remembered."

Out of the corner of her eye, Gwen saw a large angular shadow slide silently beneath them, blocking out the faint light. She leaned forward, grasping the bars of the cage, and peered through. She nudged Tiaret. "Did you see that?"

From the other cage, Sharif asked, "What was it? Is something coming after us?"

"It appeared too large to be a terodax," Tiaret said, suddenly on guard.

Gwen tried to spot the thing again and saw the silhouette eclipsing a bright patch of lava below. It came back toward them, too rectangular, too geometrical to be an aeglor or a terodax. A figure was hunched on it!

Sharif got to his feet so quickly that his cage rocked, and Vic and Lyssandra clutched each other for balance. "That is a flying carpet—a large one."

The shape came much closer, and Gwen made out the old sultan sitting on his crimson flying carpet, which was more than twice the size of Sharif's.

"Father, how did you break free?" Sharif called in a carefully lowered voice. The sultan flew up directly beneath the cages on the large rug. Gwen had seen the floor covering in his bedchamber and had thought it a normal carpet, but she should have realized it was the same one Jabir had used for their procession around the city. The intricate patterns and weavings of aja thread made the sultan's flying carpet more magnificent than the smaller purple one that Sharif used for his personal transportation.

"It is fortunate that I keep this carpet in my chambers. The aeglors did not think to search beneath a weak old man's bed for a means of escape." He indicated a curved blade that hung by his side. "And this was secreted among the heavy hangings outside my bedchamber. We must leave here. There is very little time."

"Father, are you cured?" Sharif said, and Gwen realized that the old man did indeed seem vibrant and full of energy. His eyes sparkled, his movements were quick and sure.

"I can function well enough for now," he said and rose to his feet, carefully keeping his balance. "Long enough to break you free. I must get you away from Azric ... if it is the last thing I do."

"We can travel much faster if we take two carpets," Sharif said. He quickly used the rune woven into his own flying carpet to summon it.

"Why didn't you call your carpet before?" Vic asked. "Sheesh, what were you waiting for?"

Sharif turned to him. "What good would it have done? We were still locked in the cages. If my rug flew around riderless, the aeglors or the terodax would have seized it. Now, though, we have a chance."

The sultan reached out to Sharif's cage first with a bulky set of jangling keys. His hands trembled, but he moved with determination, thrusting the key into the lock. "As sultan, I always owned a ceremonial set of keys to the Deepest Dungeon, even though I never used the cages in my reign."

"I'm glad you don't throw useless keepsakes away," Vic said.

The lock released, and the bars swung open with a rusty screech. Startled, Gwen looked around, expecting the terodax or aeglors to come and investigate. Holding on to the bars, Sharif carefully lowered himself out of the cage. Giving his father a firm, awkward hug, he said, "Now we must help my friends."

The young man glanced around for his flying carpet, which was sure to circle out of the shadows and come to get them. Gwen hoped it wouldn't race through the palace and alert the aeglors that something was up. Sharif looked into his father's eyes. "You seem much stronger."

"I needed the strength," the sultan said in a brittle voice. "I took the rest of the antidote Jabir prepared for me. All of it."

"All? But that is certainly too much. Your body cannot take it."

"My body can take very little anymore," the sultan said. "I have been on borrowed time for weeks; the antidote will keep me strong for just a little while longer."

"But when it burns out, you will have no resistance left. You will—"

"I will do what I must," the sultan said, reaching up to steady Lyssandra as she climbed down onto his carpet.

Gwen saw that, along with a curved sword, he still had his ornate flute in his sash. "How did you get away from Azric's guards, Your Majesty? I know they were watching your bedroom."

"I am old and weak. I was poisoned. They saw how little health I still had." The sultan looked over at her as Vic dropped onto the carpet. "I lay on my plush bed, coughing, the breath rattling in my throat. Because they knew I was dying and weak, they posted only two aeglor guards, and they were lax. They mocked me and thought me broken. I let them believe that. I took up my flute, just an old man wishing to play a little music in peace."

With a sly smile, he held up the flute. "It can indeed make lovely music, but after I experienced several assassination attempts, I learned clever ways to defend myself. This flute can also blow poisoned darts. I keep three stored in the mouth-piece." He wheezed and coughed, then drew a strong breath again. "I used two darts to kill my unsuspecting guards. After their bodies fell, I knew that no one would check on them, or on me, for some time. I found Jabir's antidote and consumed it all. Then, when my strength was sufficient, I moved the bed just enough to liberate my personal flying carpet. I flew out through the balcony and came to rescue you. I was unable to coordinate my efforts with Jabir, though I suspect that he is also trying to escape."

"He sent us a message of encouragement," Sharif said. "That is all we know."

"You are a formidable opponent," Tiaret said when the sultan flew to their cage and unlocked it.

"Your carpet is here, Sharif," Lyssandra said.

A smaller rectangle darted across the sky, circling to hover beside the sultan's large carpet. Sharif helped Gwen out of the iron sphere. "Come. If two of us ride on mine, my father's carpet will fly faster." The two of them climbed onto the small rug.

The sultan drew the heavy scimitar from his sash and

handed it to Sharif. "Take this for protection, my son. I am too old and weak to wield it."

As lithe as a cat, Tiaret sprang from the cage onto the sultan's carpet, while Sharif's carpet hovered beside it.

"We must head for the crystal door to Elantya," the sultan said.

"How long do you think it will take?" Gwen asked.

"Did you bring a GPS system with you, Doc? Maybe a jet engine or two?"

Suddenly they heard a loud outcry overhead, the bellows of angry aeglors.

"Sharif should be able to find the way," the sultan said.

Sharif snapped his gaze up at the rough rock base of the island over their heads. "I think someone discovered the two dead guards in your bedchamber, Father."

"I had hoped to have more time than this."

"Um, shouldn't we be leaving now?" Vic asked.

"Which direction do we go?" Gwen said. "Maybe we should make a plan in case we get separated."

"A *plan*?" Vic cried. "Distance first, planning later."

Loud horns sounded up in Irrakesh. More and more aeglors began shrieking, gathering and launching from the high towers. Below, the terodax also sounded the alarm.

Gwen could see a cloud of them, like vultures flying up from a battlefield. "This can't be good," she said.

"Follow me, Father," Sharif cried, and his small purple carpet streaked off into the night.

The sultan traced his fingers across the embroidery patterns, and his larger carpet followed Sharif's in swift pursuit. A cacophony of cries came from behind them. Gwen looked back at the enormous floating island of Irrakesh, a startling silhouette against the stars and firelight. The aeglors were searching the city, flying down streets, apparently assuming the sultan was still there, hiding in the bazaar or the lower town.

The terodax, however, flew up from the volcanic surface in a large flock of jagged wings and sharpened talons. Their scarlet-crested leader led the formation. They plunged after the two escaping flying carpets and Gwen could see they would close the distance any moment.

CHAPTER 19

Sharif looked back at Irrakesh. His city. And almost—almost—went back. Yes, his father had sacrificed everything to release the five of them from their cages. But the old man could not last long with the overdose of antidote burning through his bloodstream. No matter how much Sharif wanted to change the facts, he knew enough about poisons and the ravages the sultan's body had already suffered to understand that these were the last few moments he would have with his father. There was so much they needed to discuss, so many things to say, too much Sharif still had to learn.

And one thing he needed to know was how he, Ali el Sharif, could be responsible for the people in Irrakesh. The city had been captured by the aeglors, and who knew how many of his people had died in the attacks of the terodax? Azric would enslave and torment the survivors, and Sharif was simply running away. This could not be!

On the other hand, the five linked companions in the prophesied Ring of Might could be the only ones able to stop Azric from plundering and devastating all the worlds linked through the crystal doors. They had to get away, return to Elantya and warn others about what the dark sage was doing. The situation was desperate, but he would not give up hope. He wished Piri could be here, but he was grateful to have Gwen, Vic, Tiaret, and Lyssandra there beside him, as well as his father. He had learned to value things that were far more important than the material possessions that belonged to the leader of Irrakesh. He valued freedom and friendship.

The commotion continued in Irrakesh. Aeglors flew around the city. Someone shouted an alarm. The terodax coming up from the ground homed in on the two flying carpets. King Raathun and his winged men finally understood that the sultan had escaped, that their real target was flying away from the city.

Before the aeglors could go far, though, a small figure appeared on the palace balcony. With his sharp eyesight, Sharif recognized the pastel sunset colors of the vizier's robe. Jabir had also broken away from his captors. He cried out in defiance, his voice unusually strong. He raised his hands, and electricity bounced from fingertip to fingertip. Sharif heard the words in the ancient language, saw his gestures even from afar, and knew what the great vizier was doing—using air magic. Jabir was summoning a windstorm.

Gusts of wind blew into Sharif's face, whisking past them toward the flying city. The vizier called the breezes, streaming the air toward him to create an immense cyclone, a vortex of winds that swirled around the winged warriors. The aeglors shrieked and flapped. Their formations scattered.

The windstorm pushed King Raathun and his followers back, giving the carpets a greater lead. But the storm bought them only a minute before aeglor guards in the palace pounced on Jabir from behind and pulled him away from the balcony. His concentration broke and the spell dissolved. The winds died away and the aeglors shot toward them again with powerful strokes of their feathered wings.

Sharif could see that the terodax would arrive first. The bat-winged predators zoomed upward like airborne soldiers in tight ranks with their scarlet-crested leader at the point. The terodax leader hissed and snarled. He beat his taut wings with a sound like leather snapping against the wind.

With Gwen close behind him, Sharif pushed his flying carpet to its greatest possible speed. They streaked along, but there was nowhere to hide in the empty sky. Even if they flew all night, he doubted that his carpet could go farther than the terodax could fly in pursuit. The relentless predatory creatures would flap their wings until they dropped from exhaustion. They followed their leader in a streamlined attacking force.

On the larger carpet carrying Vic, Tiaret, and Lyssandra, the old sultan hovered over his aja thread patterns, guiding the large rug, keeping up with Sharif. Because he himself was a Key, Sharif could sense the location of the crystal door to Elantya. Unfortunately, Irrakesh had drifted a great distance after King Raathun betrayed the city and the aeglors took over. Irrakesh was too far from its usual location. The apprentices didn't stand a chance of getting back to Elantya—at least not that way.

The terodax leader dove beneath the flying carpets and put on an extra burst of speed, winging forward and upward toward the prince. The sultan pulled out his bejeweled flute. Sharif knew that his father still had one poisoned dart left in the tube, but the terodax had thick, leathery skin partially covered with scales. The bony head crest of the leader would protect it from something as small and insignificant as a needle, no matter how deadly the poison was.

Pulling closer to the purple flying carpet, the terodax leader slashed with his clawed hands, swinging his razor-edged wings. Sharif and Gwen ducked, nearly falling off the carpet. Gwen threw herself flat against the soft material. The curved wing-claw of the flying predator caught and tore the back of her blouse. The terodax leader snapped his long, jagged jaws.

Sharif gripped his father's scimitar, ready to slash the huge predator as it dove toward them on another attacking run. Another terodax followed it around in a perfectly coordinated maneuver. The other predators didn't seem to think for themselves and simply flew in the wake of their leader.

Before the scarlet-crested terodax could strike the prince's carpet again, though, the old sultan, with a last burst of energy, stood up on his rug. He shouted in a hoarse voice, raising both of his hands. "Here! Over here."

"No, Father!" Sharif shouted, but the old man called to the terodax leader.

"He is just a boy. He is nothing. I am the sultan. You want me."

The terodax leader thrashed his barbed tail and changed course. Sharif knew his father must have some intention of sacrificing himself, but the old man was no match for the terodax. What could he possibly gain? With the jeweled flute in one hand, the sultan crouched, waiting for the terodax leader to attack.

Raising the curved sword, Sharif changed course and flew toward his father.

Extending his talons, the flying monster dove down. The sultan snapped to Vic, who sat beside him looking for a way to fight to defend them. "You must pilot this rug. Fly it to safety."

"Wait a second. I've never flown one of these before—cool. Okay, I'll try to—"

"No. You will *do* it," the sultan said and abruptly turned back toward the oncoming terodax leader.

Tiaret appeared ready to throw herself upon the creature to

claw its eyes out with her own fingers if necessary. The sultan pushed her back down to the carpet.

"Here!" he shouted again at the winged predators. At the last instant, the sultan straightened, making himself a perfect target, and the clawed hands of the terodax leader snatched the old man from the large carpet and whisked him away.

Sharif cried out but could find no words. His father's lips were drawn back in a snarl as the terodax leader lifted him toward his jagged jaws. The sultan raised the jeweled flute, somehow managing to aim, and blew a sharp burst of air through the tube. At point-blank range, the last poisoned dart struck the soft, vulnerable tissue in the terodax leader's mouth.

The creature squealed, flexing its clawed hands. Sharif's father grabbed on to the talons, refusing to let the thing drop him. Crying out and hissing, the flying predator spiraled down. The poison worked swiftly. Shrieking in agony, the terodax leader lost altitude.

"Live well, my son," the sultan cried with his last breath.

When the poison reached the terodax leader's brain, its wings twitched spasmodically, but it could no longer fly. As the leader plummeted away from the flying carpets, the rest of the winged creatures blindly flew after it, following their king down.

In the darkness, Sharif quickly lost sight of his father.

CHAPTER 20

Vic could hear Sharif cry out in hopeless anguish at his father's death. At the same time, the flock of attacking terodax peeled away in pursuit of their dying leader. But Vic could only concentrate on trying to fly the magic carpet. He wished he had some kind of user's manual— then again, he rarely wasted time reading directions. He traced the lines of embroidery with his fingers, struggling to summon his own magic and remember what he had picked up from Sharif in Elantya and the vizier here in Irrakesh.

Sure, he could do this. If he couldn't, they would all crash to the ground far below. So he was inclined to experiment. He quickly figured out which patterns caused the rug to move from side to side, to dip sickeningly downward or to pull up in a steep ascent. It all made sense, in a way, and flying this carpet was much simpler than some of the complex video games he had played back at home. No problem.

Well, there *was* a problem, now that he saw the aeglors flying behind them and closing the distance.

"The terodax are returning," Lyssandra said, pointing down.

Tiaret stood, bracing her feet on the rug's soft surface. "And the aeglors will be here within moments."

Gwen had her arm around Sharif's waist. The young man stoically focused on his carpet, guiding them onward.

"How much farther to the door, Sharif?" Vic called. "Can we get there?"

Sharif looked back at him. They were racing neck and neck, but they could hear the hundreds of winged warriors of both species coming onward angrily. "It would take us half a day to reach it."

Lyssandra's long, coppery hair blew about her face in the winds. "Even on Elantya, we must take a long ocean voyage to get to the proper location."

Vic took the carpet to its top speed. He looked back at all of the aeglors in a great mass, their weapons clutched tightly in their hands. From below came the scattered and chaotic group of leaderless terodax. They no longer flew in formation, but Vic was sure they could be dangerous, even without specific orders.

Azric had had enough control over the terodax leader to keep the creatures from killing the five friends. Now that their leader was dead, though, Vic didn't think the winged predators would have any compunction against tearing the apprentices to pieces. On the other hand, it might be worse if they were captured again by the aeglors and dragged back to Azric. The very fate of worlds depended on this.

"If I had my teaching staff or even my quarterstaff," Tiaret said, "I would make a brave accounting for our lives."

"And if I had a rocket," Vic said, "I could blast us out of here faster than those things could follow."

"If wishes were horses, then beggars would ride," Gwen said.

"Thanks, Doc. Is quoting nursery rhymes really the most useful thing you can do right now?" Vic yelled. Suddenly it hit him. *He* could do something more useful. "Wait. If we can't get to the actual crystal door, couldn't I create a new one—if I remember how?"

"Of course you can!" Gwen cried. "Just focus, Dr. Distracto. Get us out of here."

Vic took a deep breath. The aeglors were approaching in a thunder of feathers, and the squawking terodax rattled his concentration. But Vic had to do it—create a new crystal door up here in the middle of the sky. *This* was his special ability as part of the Ring of Might.

"The moment you open the doorway, we must fly through it, Viccus," Tiaret said. "I will use my power to slam it shut. We cannot allow the aeglors or terodax to follow."

"Hurry," Lyssandra said.

Vic concentrated. He pictured his fellow apprentices and thought of their urgent need to warn his father, Ven Sage Rubicas, and the Pentumvirate. What the friends needed was a secret passageway back to Elantya. They had to get from here to there right away.

As soon as the sparkling hole opened in the air, Sharif's purple carpet streaked through the opening. Gwen held on to the fringe of gold tassels.

"Here we go," Vic said, urging the larger carpet through. Vic saw pale dawn light and puffy clouds, a rising sun glittering off a smooth ocean. It was a different time of day in a different world. And below them was the coastline of an island studded with buildings, a harbor full of ships.

"Bull's-eye!" he said. "I got us right over Elantya."

At the back of the rug, Tiaret faced the impromptu crystal door. She raised her arms and made a flinging motion, as if heaving a massive gate shut. The crystal door shimmered and vanished as if it had never existed.

Thinking fast, Gwen yanked open a window to watch what was happening behind them.

In the night sky of the other world, King Raathun and his many muscular warriors put on a burst of speed. They might not understand how, but they seemed to sense that the five companions were about to escape. A few of the violent and unsettled terodax crashed into the lead aeglors, and a brawl ensued. Raathun seemed to be bellowing at them.

Several aeglors and terodax fell, still slashing with swords and battering with clubs. Raathun, in the lead, swept through the space where the rugs had been moments ago. In the silent image, the king of the aeglors let out an enraged cry.

Gwen let the window close.

Vic wanted to collapse with relief, jump up and down, and shout all at the same time. Sharif, however, looking stricken and grim, flew directly down toward Elantya without a word. Vic followed him. He knew they were safe for the time being, but Elantya was still in great danger.

CHAPTER 21

After the escaped apprentices arrived back in Elantya, essential personnel from all over the island were hastily summoned to a meeting in the Pentumvirate Hall. Gwen was glad to see everyone arrive so quickly. Vir Questas brought the apprentices' crystal daggers with him and also returned the unbreakable teaching staff to the girl from Afirik. Tiaret spent the rest of the short wait in serious conversation with Questas and the raven-and-gold-haired Helassa, no doubt briefing them on the various forms of attack Azric could now bring to bear.

When Groxas, Kaisa, and Xandas got there, they headed straight for Lyssandra and enveloped her in a warm family embrace. Admiral Bradsinoreus entered the rotunda with a cluster of his captains. Uncle Cap arrived shortly thereafter, followed by the clanking walker forms of anemonite Sages Polup and Gedup, along with the rebel merlon Ulbar and a handful of his scaly companions. Dr. Pierce rushed to throw his arms around Gwen and Vic and refused to leave their sides even when Vir Etherya called the meeting to order.

Watching Sharif standing erect, silent, proud, and utterly alone, his left hand resting on the hilt of his father's curved sword, Gwen reflected on the absolute cruelty of a fate that had given him so much and taken away even more. The death of his mother, the murder of his brother, and the indifference of his father and sisters had shaped the young man's personality. He had built a fortress around his feelings and only gradually allowed a few friends in to see who he really was. Then Piri had been snatched from him in the lavaja fields, presumed murdered by Orpheon, after which the merlons had proceeded to break down the prince's haughty, protective facade.

The emotional roller coaster had continued with Piri's return and the apprentices' escape from the merlons. Through all of that, Sharif had grown and changed. Then, shortly after learning that he was truly part of something greater than himself, Piri had been taken from him again. And at the very moment that the sultan had undeniably proved his love for his son, Sharif had lost him forever. Gwen had wept for Sharif and with him—a luxury she had rarely allowed herself—and she wondered how he could hold up under the strain. But when his olive eyes met hers, she saw the strength there.

He moved closer to her on the side opposite Cap and took her hand, and suddenly Gwen understood that her friend's silence was not part of the fortress he had once built around himself. It was part of the chrysalis in which he was being transformed from boy to man. She also understood that she, Vic, Lyssandra, and Tiaret had been undergoing similar changes, undeniable transformations.

Gwen forced her mind back to the current urgent situation. Vic was just finishing an overview of what had taken place in Irrakesh. Gwen quickly described for the Virs how she and Vic had "forged" a Ring of Might and that they had already discovered some useful new skills. Sharif filled in details of his father's death, and Lyssandra talked about their escape.

"So," Vic concluded, "Azric's going to pull in all of his allies to attack Elantya by sea and land *and* air. We know for certain that he'll have aeglors, terodax, all of the merlons, and any creatures they've enslaved."

"Not all," Ulbar said. "Many merlons do not follow mad King Barak, and as for his planned attack from the foundations of Elantya, the anemonites and my people have removed every lavaja bomb from the catacombs beneath the island. That is one danger at least that we do not face."

"Even so," Tiaret said, "I believe Azric means to attack soon, within a few days at the most."

"That is a sensible estimate." Ulbar rippled his head fin. "My scouts report large numbers of Barak's warrior merlons on the move already."

"How can we be certain of the timing?" Vir Helassa asked.

"My spies cannot risk revealing themselves too soon, but they will find a way to warn us when the merlon attack is imminent."

Vir Pecunyas cleared his throat. "But what of Azric's flying armies? Will they arrive before, after, or *with* the merlons?"

"Maybe we can find out what they're saying." Gwen motioned up into the air, and a window appeared that showed Azric with several terodax and the king of the aeglors.

After listening intently for several seconds, Lyssandra relayed their words.

"It is time to bring in the rest of your men," Azric said. "I want them all ready by the time the city is in position by the crystal door tomorrow. We will launch the aerial attacks from here directly through the door. I could transform myself into an aeglor or terodax, of course, but I believe my present form is more likely to strike terror into the hearts of the sages. I am, after all, the most powerful wizard who ever lived."

The terodax and King Raathun swept their wings wide in salute and took off while Azric tapped the tips of his fingers lazily together. Gwen let the window close.

"This matter is urgent," Bradsinoreus said, stepping forward. "We must not allow Azric's forces to reach Elantya by air, if it can be helped. They will be far more difficult to defeat. At present, however, they are bottled up in another world."

"And the neck of that bottle is the crystal door itself," Tiaret said.

"So, head 'em off at the pass, huh?" Vic asked. "Kinda has a ring to it."

"But be warned," Tiaret said, "I can close the door, but as long as Azric has a Key, he can open it again and again."

"Even so," Bradsinoreus said, "we can more effectively defend ourselves *at* the crystal door than by waiting for all of our enemies to come to Elantya."

The rose decision crystals on the Vir's carved stone chairs lit in unanimous agreement.

The gold-robed Vir of Resources looked at the other members of the council. "Then it is decided?" Parsimanias said in his clipped voice.

Vir Etherya's expression was grave. "Yes. The Pentumvirate will take this fight to the crystal door."

"Ven Rubicas, we will need you and your apprentices," Vir Questas said.

Helassa shook her head with impatience. "We must bring *all* of our brightest sages, our bravest fighters, our most powerful weapons. By containing our enemies at that crystal door, we will not have to fight them in Elantya." Vir Helassa stood. "Alert the fleet, Admiral. We leave at sunset."

On their way to prepare for their journey, Vic and Gwen stopped by Kyara's tank with Vic's father, who had been immersed in his defense projects. Vic knew that he, Sage Groxas, and the anemonites had been working hard on several kinds of weapons. His dad's design for the pistol-sized crossbow called an arrow-pult was popular among civilians. His team had also augmented Polup's Grogyptian Fire cannon, produced hundreds of the weapons, and installed them in several war galleys, in the cliffs on the northern boundary of the harbor, and at other strategic places around Elantya.

"I'm afraid we haven't had as much time to spend on Kyara as I'd have liked," Vic's father admitted. "But think about it—if we don't save Elantya, we'll lose Kyara, too."

"I know, Dad. Elantya first, Mom later." Vic put his hand in the water and touched the ice coral. "I miss you, Mom. I'm sorry we struck out in Irrakesh. I was hoping that the Air Spirits would be more helpful or that we'd find a clue in the Grand Library."

"Don't worry, son," Dr. Pierce said. "We've got a lot more tricks up our sleeves than you think. A bunch of us sages and anemonites brainstormed and came up with a list of possible solutions to this problem. We're only a third of the way through that list."

Vic could feel inside him that they would find a way to solve the problem, once Elantya was safe. He gave his dad an encouraging grin.

Gwen said, "Who knows? Since Taz and I are the children of the prophecy, maybe once this is all over we'll learn that one of our new talents is thawing ice coral."

Vic shrugged. "Why not? Stranger things have happened. Now let's go put a serious kink in Azric's plans."

CHAPTER 22

While the ships prepared to leave at sunset, Gwen and her friends offered to fly patrol around the island on the two magic carpets. Lyssandra and Tiaret flew with Vic on the larger carpet, while Gwen rode with Sharif.

Since the five had hurried back to Elantya and sounded a warning, the already frenetic defensive preparations had gone into overdrive in addition to the battle fleet being readied for departure. Lookout towers flashed signals with quicksilver mirrors and wind crystals.

"We've got company," Vic said. "Look." He pointed down toward some wavelets well beyond the breakwater, a thick spit of stacked rocks and packed gravel that extended along the outer edge of the deep harbor.

Gwen nibbled at the edge of her lower lip. "Could Azric have gotten here this fast?"

"Not a chance," Vic said, but his voice was not as certain as his words.

"And Ulbar said his people would send warning, if the

merlons were making an all-out assault on the island," Lyssandra said.

"We must prepare, nonetheless," Tiaret replied. "I am glad to have my teaching staff again."

Gwen saw the smooth waves begin to churn outside the harbor. Not far below the five friends, a group of scaly creatures lifted their fin-fringed heads into the air. Their thick-lipped mouths were filled with needle teeth. The merlon warriors bobbed in the water, peering around with wide, slitted eyes.

Sharif and Vic both took their carpets into a sharp climb and hovered high above, watching from a safer distance.

"Good idea," Gwen said. Tiaret gripped her teaching staff, as if wishing she were close enough for hand-to-hand combat.

Farther out in the water, a sinuous, curving head broke the surface and rose up like the towering neck of a dragon. Gwen groaned. They had battled the merlons' giant sea serpents before. "Why aren't they doing anything?" she asked.

From a pocket, Lyssandra pulled a spell scroll that she had brought for the fight at the crystal door. She read it quickly and said, *"S'ibah."* When Vic raised a questioning eyebrow at her, she explained, "Translation spell. I thought it best that all of us be able to understand what the merlons say."

A gaudily armored merlon male rode a metal plate attached to a chainmail harness on the back of the lead sea serpent, a green-scaled monster with black leopard spots. Six more sea monsters rose up, each carrying another heavily armed warrior. High-ranking merlons, Gwen guessed.

"There is King Barak," Sharif said, putting a hand to the curved sword at his side. "I would recognize that mad merlon anywhere."

"We've had more than enough of that nutcase," Vic said.

Tiaret pointed to a sleek female merlon who carried a

pointed trident in her grip. "And Goldskin. I had hoped for a second chance to defeat her."

"You've got to be kidding." Vic snorted. "*I* hoped I'd never see her again."

"Or any merlons," Gwen added.

Triangular fins sliced like daggers through the waves as sharks circled. A merlon army had indeed arrived—threatening, but not the overwhelming force Gwen had expected for the grand attack.

Though the merlons had brought a great deal of pain and death to the people of Elantya, Gwen could not hate the entire aquatic race. The merlon king was fanatical, but kindly Ulbar had shown them that not all merlons had been corrupted by Azric. Not every sea-dweller wanted to destroy the island of Elantya and kill all air-breathers.

Holding high a long scepter crowned with a spiny metal-plated sea urchin, Barak bellowed in a threatening voice, his words burbling and hissing, "Elantya will fall. We will blast it apart, tear your buildings down, drop every rock into the water. You are all doomed."

The merlon soldiers swam closer to the breakwater barrier.

"We must fight them if they attempt to go ashore," Tiaret said.

But Barak did not order a full-fledged attack.

"Azric will soon return," the king said. "You cannot stand against our combined strength."

Gwen looked at her cousin and the other apprentices. "So the question is, why didn't he wait? Why is Barak here *now*?"

"Tactically, his actions are unwise," Tiaret said.

"I think he's grandstanding," Vic said. "He hates sitting around twiddling his fins. He knows Azric is coming, and he wanted to get a head start by trying to scare us."

"King Barak is impatient," Sharif agreed.

Gwen could easily imagine the merlon king not being able to wait for the appointed day. Full of bluster and threats, he had rounded up sea serpents, sharks, and warriors and come here to beat his chest. She shook her head in disbelief. "Like a kid trying to open his birthday presents ahead of time."

Vic laughed. "And you call *me* Doctor Distracto."

Riding high on his sea serpent, Barak waved his sea-urchin scepter in the air. "When Azric arrives, all land-dwellers will perish. We merlons will reclaim our world. Prepare to meet your doom."

Vic gagged. "I've read better evil-genius speeches in comic books."

"I have dreamed of great battles," Lyssandra said. "There are more to come, but this ... this is not the time."

Suddenly, a commotion occurred farther out in the water behind Barak's massed merlons. Many more merlons surfaced in ranks, rising up in lines of heavily armed warriors that advanced toward the rear of Barak's undersea soldiers. Slippery black whales slowly breached, curling upward and extending their thick fins above the water. Four of the black whales rolled in unison and slapped their fins down in a thunderous splash.

"Uh-oh. Reinforcements," Gwen said. "Now we're in deep trouble."

"No—not reinforcements," Sharif corrected. "Those are merlon rebels." A black-and-white orca surfaced with a merlon on its back, holding the dorsal fin. "And that is Ulbar."

"Not all merlons follow you, Barak," Ulbar shouted. "You have oppressed our cities and sold the honor of Szishh to a tyrant. We will defend ourselves and Elantya against you. We have many spies in your armies, Barak. We know your every move."

The opposing merlons eyed each other warily. Barak whirled

his sea serpent and waved his urchin scepter in the air. "Traitors! You will all be crushed."

"Rout out the spies in your midst—if you can," Ulbar challenged. The whales thrashed, demonstrating the merlon rebels' readiness to clash with Barak's army.

"Why would Ulbar reveal that his own people are among Barak's merlons?" Lyssandra wondered out loud.

Tiaret gave a knowing smile. "It is brilliant. Although Ulbar has only a few spies with Barak, he knows that the merlon king is paranoid. Now Barak will suspect each of his generals, every one of his fighters."

Vic and Gwen chuckled at the ingenious tactic.

As the slick-skinned whales careened forward, Barak's scaly soldiers prepared to fight them. At Ulbar's command, the whales rose up and turned their blowholes toward the towering sea serpents and the merlon commanders riding them. With a sudden, unexpected blast, the whales shot a furious stream of spray that struck Barak squarely, knocking him off of his saddle-throne and backward into the water.

The serpentine necks of the sea monsters drew back from the continued water blasts. The whales submerged again to refill and came up to spray their adversaries again and again. Gold-skin and the other merlon generals were unseated from their sea serpents as well. Barak came up, looking flustered and affronted.

"Water does not harm merlons," Tiaret pointed out with bafflement.

"No," Gwen said, "but Barak is obviously humiliated."

The merlon king apparently had no stomach for a fight now that Ulbar and his rebels had arrived and the odds were against him. Barak clutched his leopard-spotted sea serpent and shouted again, "Azric is coming. We will grind your island to rubble. I will find the spies in my midst. Then we will hunt down and kill every merlon traitor."

The whales blasted him with another fusillade from their water cannons. The sea serpents ducked under the water, and the attacking merlons submerged, following their leader's retreat.

Ulbar and his rebels swam patrol, guarding the harbor. The apprentices watched for any further surprises, but the waves grew calm. Barak and his merlons had indeed withdrawn ... for now.

"Trust me, that was only a warm-up act," Vic said.

"For us, too," Sharif said, looking grim.

"We'd better get on those ships and head for the crystal door," Gwen said. "Azric is on his way."

CHAPTER 23

As the fleet of war galleys approached the crystal door to Irrakesh, Gwen felt the pressure building in her. Sages Snigmythya, Abakas, Polup, and a score of others were distributed on various ships throughout the fleet. Her cousin and Uncle Cap, Lyssandra and her parents, and Tiaret were on the nearby galley *Thunder Shield* with Ven Sage Rubicas. Vic had the large magic carpet with them, and Sharif had his own smaller carpet at the ready.

Gwen and Sharif waved periodically, and Gwen knew that if she needed to, she could write notes to them, since she and Vic had both brought along the miniature magical notebooks that the Virs had given them. Skrits and aquits traveled from ship to ship carrying messages that did not need to be instantaneous.

Ulbar and his helpful merlons swam with the fleet, keeping watch for any enemies approaching from beneath. At the suggestion of Sage Pierce, several galleys had been fitted with transparent view ports beneath the water level. The ports were made of similar material to that used in Ven Sage Rubicas's aquariums, but Cap and the anemonites had reinforced it to withstand greater pressure.

With Admiral Bradsinoreus and so many sages, merlons, and Pentumvirate members in the war fleet, as well as the Ring of Might, Gwen thought she should feel at least slightly safer. But there was no safety in war, and she and her friends were on the front lines.

Not only that, but phrases from the prophecies kept popping into her head—things like "Two shall seal the tyrant's doom" and "Pledged to serve and to protect" and "Leaving evil no retreat"—reminding Gwen that she and her cousin and the rest of the Ring had a crucial role to play if Azric was to be defeated. "The Virs claim that this is the final battle—they're going to vanquish Azric once and for all."

Standing beside her at the rail of the *Bright Warrior*, Sharif said, "It is good that they have finally decided to act first rather than wait to be attacked."

Suck it up, Pierce, Gwen chided herself silently. *Billions of people in hundreds of worlds are counting on you. Right—no pressure there.* Aloud, she said to Sharif, "I suppose so. Do you feel ready?"

Giving her a wry look, he answered, "Other than the fact that I have no idea what my special power is? Yes—what choice do we have?"

He was right, of course. She blew out a quick breath and composed herself. "I guess giving in to doubt at a time like this would only be self-indulgence."

He raised an eyebrow and gave her an approving look. "I believe my people could make a saying from those words."

Without further discussion, the two apprentices headed toward the prow of the ship where Admiral Bradsinoreus was discussing strategy with Virs Helassa and Parsimanias. Each Vir held a basket of spell scrolls arranged in a strategic order as to when they believed they would need them.

"Do you have weapons?" Helassa asked. "The daggers I gave you?"

Gwen pulled out her dagger and flashed it at the Vir of Protection. Sharif hefted his scimitar and indicated the arrow-pult clipped to the sash at his waist. Most of the civilians and apprentices carried these hand weapons now. This seemed to distress Bradsinoreus. "Let us hope it does not come to that. We have a full complement of archers aboard this ship, not to mention dozens of neosages and journeysages to assist us."

Sharif shook his head slowly. "Everyone must be ready. Azric always has more tricks than one can anticipate. He even captured Piri."

Gwen could tell that this warning made little impact on the admiral, who was, after all, a man of great confidence, action, and competence. He did not expect to lose.

"Sharif is right," she said. "Every person on every ship in this fleet should be prepared to fight whatever comes through that crystal door."

"I would rather that our civilian support personnel did not fight," Bradsinoreus said.

"Admiral," Helassa said, giving him a stern but not unkind look, "there are no longer any 'civilians' in Elantya. Anyone who did not wish to face the enemy was sent to safety through one of the crystal doors. Those who remain—they are our army."

When the ships finally arrived at the door to Irrakesh, they arranged themselves in a defensive formation. Gwen immediately opened a window into the other world to see what Azric and his armies were doing. Although she wasn't conscious of how exactly she controlled her skill, Gwen managed to make a window large enough for everyone in the fleet to see, hovering above the lead ship like the screen in a movie theater. The process felt as natural to her as breathing.

In the image, thousands of winged creatures, both feathered

and leathery, flocked their way above an expanse of sand. "They will be here soon," Sharif said. "The place in that image is only a few minutes' journey from the door, if I were flying the distance on my carpet."

Sharif uttered a curse under his breath as an aeglor flew into view carrying Vizier Jabir, bound hand and foot, bruised, and bleeding from several shallow cuts on his head—obvious signs of his torture. Azric rode a giant terodax beside the aeglor. Piri's glowing bottle-prison was tied to his sash, and he shouted something to his winged armies.

On the *Thunder Shield* not far from the *Bright Warrior*, Lyssandra reported Azric's speech to Ven Sage Rubicas while Vic scribbled what she said in his small notebook. From her own notebook, Gwen read the words that appeared as fast as Vic could transcribe what Lyssandra was telling him. Prepare the Key. Today another world becomes ours.

Knowing that the first stage of the plan involved her friend from Afirik, Gwen jotted the words, Luck to Tiaret. From the other ship, Vic waved and then passed his cousin's message to the warrior girl as she stepped forward.

"Only another minute or so," Sharif said, tracking the army's approach.

"Could we not simply keep the door closed?" Vir Parsimanias asked.

"I don't think so," Gwen said. "Vic can create doors and Tiaret slams them. I can see through to other worlds, and Lyssandra can hear them, but so far none of us knows how to *keep* a door shut."

"Even if we could, my people and Piri are captives of the dark sage. I would not wish to leave them trapped with such evil," Sharif pointed out. "I must find a way to save them."

"The army has arrived," Vir Parsimanias said.

Bradsinoreus signaled the other ships.

Flying in place, the aeglor holding Jabir wrapped his leg talons around the vizier and squeezed hard. Azric shouted something to Jabir, or perhaps it was to the aeglor. The aeglor squeezed harder and small spots of blood appeared on the vizier's sunset-streaked robes. At last, a doorway opened, sparkling like a spray of shattered glass. Aeglors and terodax dove toward it. They were almost there, when—

Tiaret slammed the door in their faces. In Gwen's window image, the swooping fighters fluttered in confusion as they soared aimlessly through open air where the crystal door had been just a second ago. Gwen was finding the viewing window hard to keep open so long. A flash of annoyance crossed Azric's face and Gwen struggled to hold the connection of the window. At another shouted order from the dark sage, the door opened again, and again Tiaret slammed it before the airborne combatants could pass through.

This continued three more times until Bradsinoreus said, "Confusion has gained us all the advantage we could have hoped for. But now we must fight."

"Let the door remain open," Helassa agreed. "Perhaps when they get through, they will let the Key go." She waved to Tiaret to stop, and the girl from Afirik stepped back from the prow of the *Thunder Shield*.

Although she must have been tired from repeatedly using her door-closing powers, Tiaret raised her teaching staff overhead and spun it a few times, signaling that she was more than prepared for the fight.

The door opened again. As if he knew that the battle was finally at hand, the Azric in the image sneered down at Piri's purple and amber bottle. Then he smiled and barked a silent order. The massive terodax he rode dove toward the door and plunged through with countless terodax and aeglors following.

Exhausted, Gwen let her window fall shut. Helassa and

Parsimanias unrolled the first of their spell scrolls while Bradsinoreus signaled orders to the other ships. Gwen held an arrowpult in one hand and her crystal dagger in the other. Beside her, Sharif raised his curved blade.

The great battle with Azric had come.

CHAPTER 24

From three separate war galleys, the five members of the Pentumvirate read spell scrolls, combining their skills. They faced the stream of terodax and aeglors that rushed at the ships through the crystal door from Sharif's world. Lyssandra, who had been translating what was being said in Gwen's window, suddenly felt dizzy and weak. Flashes of waves and sea serpents, merlons and flying creatures, ships and flying carpets, and embattled Virs and sages strobed in her mind's eye. She reached out and grabbed Vic's hand. "Today will bring great sadness, Viccus."

"Don't worry, Lyssandra," Vic said, steadying her. "I'll try to be your knight in shining armor—or pantaloons, at least." He gave her a cockeyed grin, tugging at his loose, billowing pants. "I'll do my best."

"As will I." Taking a deep drink of greenstepe from the ever-replenishing vial that hung from a long chain around her neck, Lyssandra felt the energy returning to her. She passed the vial of greenstepe to Tiaret, who had used a great deal of energy slamming the crystal door. "I am not done fighting yet."

After drinking, Tiaret handed the vial back to Lyssandra. "I am always ready to be put to the test," she said, hefting her teaching staff and indicating the arrowpult clipped to her waistband. "I will find a good enemy for my first target today."

"You'll have plenty to choose from," Vic said, rolling out the sultan's large carpet. "Let's go."

Lyssandra's parents had gone aft with Sages Polup and Pierce to prime the cannons. Everyone was prepared to do their part. The winged men and the monstrous-looking terodax kept swooping through the gaping crystal door from the skies in front of Irrakesh and over the waters of the ocean.

Vic traced the embroidery on the carpet, and it lifted into the air, giving the friends a dauntingly clear view of the approaching attackers.

Azric rode proudly on the back of the largest terodax Lyssandra had ever seen. This one had an even broader wingspan than the terodax leader that the old sultan had killed with a poison dart. With that leader gone, Azric had no doubt taken over as "flock commander," or whatever the terodax called their main general. Though the winged predators had a vaguely human appearance despite their batlike wings, Azric rode this one as if it were a mere beast of burden. She knew the dark sage would enslave any living being—including humans—without compunction, so long as it served his purposes. She shuddered to think what might be happening in the flying city of Irrakesh under his oppressive rule.

As hundreds and hundreds of aeglors led by King Raathun, along with Azric's sharp-winged terodax, flowed through the crystal gateway, the passage remained open between the worlds.

"Tiaret, can you not slam the crystal door so no more of them can come through?" Lyssandra asked. The carpet rose higher.

The dark-skinned girl shook her head, the muscles in her jaw standing out as she clenched her teeth with effort. "I cannot. It seems that while a living thing is passing through, a crystal door cannot be closed."

"If only we knew how to seal it," Lyssandra said with dismay. "Though that would mean stranding the people of Irrakesh."

"Not necessarily," Vic said, flying the carpet in a wide arc around the fleet of battleships. "I could always rip open a new doorway, if I had to—I already did it once. Then we could free all of—"

Tiaret's golden eyes flashed. "Let us complete this battle before we contemplate others."

From the ships below, volleys of arrows shot up into the sky, some of them flaming. Because the winged warriors of both species were so thick in the air, each pointed barb found a target. Aeglors and terodax dropped into the water, many of them already dead; others thrashed and quickly drowned, the aeglors in particular. Once their thick feathers were drenched, they could no longer remain afloat.

"Sheesh," Vic said. "Good thing we weren't close enough to those flyers to get shot! We'd better stay out of the main line of fire." He watched an aeglor fall, its wings ablaze. "And I mean 'line of fire' literally."

King Raathun roared, rallying his fighters. They winged down.

A few of the fighters tried to circle around the ships to attack from the flank, and Tiaret and Lyssandra shot at them with their arrowpults.

Directed by Master Polup, cannons blasted from the ships up into the largest mass of aeglors in the sky, belching forth blue-white fire—a combination of magic and complex chemistry the anemonites had developed. Coordinating their reading with signal flags between the galleys, the Pentumvirate members recited from spell scrolls, launching powerful magical volleys.

They struck the flying attackers with the Bubble of Death spell, crackling balls of electrical fire, poisonous gases, and furious bursts of cyclone winds.

The winged army swiftly lost its military formation and attacked in a complete chaotic melee. Lyssandra thought this was what the aeglors had wanted most anyway. More arrows shot upward. Lyssandra had brought an extra basket of quarrels with them on the carpet, but now as she watched clusters of flyers circling around Azric's monstrous main force, she wondered if they had brought enough quarrels along, even if every one found a target.

As the battle continued, Lyssandra saw the horned head of a large armored sea serpent break the surface of the ocean. A single merlon soldier rode on its back.

"Shut the door now, Tiaret," Lyssandra said.

"Sheesh, talk about closing the barn door after all the horses are gone," Vic said, taking a shot at a stray terodax. "Most of them are *here* now. Why would—"

"To cut off their retreat and reinforcements," Tiaret answered. She went silent with concentration, but a few terodax stragglers were already sweeping through the crystal door, winging out of the sky from another world and sweeping low, reacting to the moist air, the cooler temperature.

The sea serpent streaked toward the sparkling portal. From their previous trip, Lyssandra knew that on the other side of the barrier, the rippling, deep-blue ocean met with an expansive wasteland of rounded sand dunes. She looked around frantically, expecting other merlons, but saw only the single sea serpent.

"That monster is heading toward the crystal door," she said.

"Well, it's in for a surprise if it tries to swim across that desert," Vic said.

The sea serpent raced forward, leaving behind a white foamy wake.

A lone terodax dove toward them, and Tiaret got to her feet on the carpet to meet it with several furious blows from her teaching staff.

Lyssandra suddenly realized what the sea serpent down below meant to do. "It will beach itself and be stranded halfway through the crystal door."

Vic attempted to evade the attacking monster without unbalancing his friends. "Slam the door now, Tiaret," he yelled.

The girl from Afirik tried, but she still battled the sharp-winged terodax. Controlling the carpet with one hand, Vic brought up his arrowpult with the other and shot at it.

Meanwhile, the sea serpent, having built up a great momentum, threw itself forward.

Apparently, Gwen had seen what was happening from her spot on Sharif's carpet—just above the *Bright Warrior*—and quickly opened a large window. Through it, Lyssandra saw the front half of the sea serpent flop onto the arid sands, while the other half stayed in the ocean.

It thrashed and writhed, between two worlds, sacrificed to keep the door open. Its raw, flapping gills quickly became coated with dust. If it stayed where it was, it would die in a matter of hours. The merlon warrior that had goaded it sprang away before he could be crushed in the sea serpent's thrashings. The merlon appeared to be panicked by the sudden dryness of the dunes. He stumbled forward, trying to brush abrasive sand from his wet skin. Gasping, he fell to his scaly knees, crawled back to the edge of the crystal door, and dragged himself over the threshold into the oceans of his own world again.

The sea serpent, though, was trapped like a beached whale on the sands, effectively jamming open the crystal door so that Azric could pass back and forth as he pleased.

Seeing that Tiaret was still struggling with the terodax, Lyssandra drew her crystal knife, stood, and plunged it into the creature's eye. It soon stopped moving and fell heavily onto the carpet, weighing them down and making the rug wobble precariously. The carpet sank toward the waves until Lyssandra and Tiaret heaved the terodax off the side into the ocean.

The giant terodax that carried Azric flapped its sail-like wings and circled high over the war galleys.

"I have waited thousands of years for this," Azric cried, his voice magically amplified to carry on the ocean air. "Surrender now or die. In either case, I will crush Elantya. Make no mistake, I *will* break the seals to free my armies. My loyal generals have waited millennia for their victory. Soon all worlds will bow to us."

The Pentumvirate members worked their spell scrolls, keeping up the defense. King Raathun brought his aeglors together, flying above the decks of the war galleys. Each aeglor dropped a large spiked ball that crashed into the decks, smashing anyone who happened to be in the way.

Vic turned the carpet toward the *Thunder Shield.*

Lyssandra saw her bearded father roll one of his small casks to a catapult launcher on the deck. Vic's father helped him secure the launcher. They aimed up in the sky as arrows continued to arc upward, killing some of the smaller aeglors and one terodax. Azric appeared to scoff at the Elantyan fleet and its weapons. Groxas and Dr. Pierce aimed and launched.

The target came close as Azric guided his terodax steed toward the ships. The dark sage held on with one hand, then raised his other, starting to work a spell. Vic's father let loose the catapult and Groxas worked an ignition spell. The small canister flew upward and Azric swerved his terodax so that they wouldn't be struck directly. But the sky fireworks exploded close by. Chunks of shrapnel and bright-colored flames and sparks blew outward, striking the terodax in its chest, shredding its wings and setting them on fire.

Even Azric was surprised. The terodax's ribs were smashed. It opened and closed its long, jagged jaws, gasping, flailing as it plummeted into the water. Lyssandra could see it was already dead. Azric fell off. Transforming in midair into a sleek diving bird, he plunged at full speed into the water.

The Virs and Elantyan sailors let out a cheer at seeing Azric fall from his steed. The aeglors shrieked with fury and renewed their attack. The terodax dropped down and began pelting the soldiers on the war galleys. The sages renewed their spells, while the archers shot even more arrows.

"Good shot, Dad," Vic cried, bringing the carpet down on the deck. Lyssandra grabbed two more baskets of arrowpult quarrels.

"That was even more effective than I expected," Groxas said. "Quick, load more sky fireworks."

"Did Azric flee?" Tiaret asked. "I wished to fight him myself."

"Trust me, he's not gone yet," Vic said. "We know he does just fine in the ocean."

Lyssandra ran to the edge of the galley and searched for any sign of Azric resurfacing but did not see the dark sage. A few dark heads emerged from the water—Ulbar's rebels signaling danger.

Just then, a guard who had been watching the viewports below decks appeared and shouted, "Merlons!"

Vic sighed. "This is going to be a long day."

CHAPTER 25

Merlons streaked toward the war galleys. Lyssandra, Tiaret, and Vic got back on the carpet and took off, readying their arrowpults and crystal daggers, as well as the spears they had gotten from the Elantyan navy. Hovering at the side of the ship below the deck level, they shot quarrels at the scaly undersea warriors who began to scramble up the rough hulls of the galleys. The merlons hissed, clawing with their webbed hands.

Vic jabbed with a spear, striking the hard seashell armor the lead merlon wore on his shoulders. The wound he inflicted was not serious, but the force was enough to send the slippery aquatic creature back into the waves.

Tiaret swung her teaching staff, knocking another merlon off the hull. Lyssandra drew a deep breath.

"Why do I feel like I've been here before?" Vic muttered.

In a burst of spray, a blunt-nosed sea serpent rose above the waves with a drenched and defiant Azric—back in human form —holding onto its horns for balance. He didn't seem to care whether he rode a sea serpent or a flying terodax. He raised his hand and shouted a command.

Now, dozens of armored sea serpents appeared all around the Elantyan war galleys in the water. An army of sharks accompanied them. Wave after wave of merlon warriors emerged. General Goldskin rode her own monstrous steed, and King Barak led them all. The merlons and their sea monsters closed in on the Elantyan navy. Aeglors and terodax dashed down from the sky, renewing their attack.

Groxas and Dr. Pierce rolled out small casks of explosives, touching their ignition runes and dropping them over the side into the water. Groxas had used the sea fireworks before to provide a diversion when the companions were rescued from the merlon city.

Though the merlons were momentarily stunned, Goldskin shouted, driving her armored sea serpents forward to continue the attack. Vic quickly raised the carpet out of the serpent's reach.

On the *Thunder Shield*, Ven Sage Rubicas read from a fresh spell scroll and created a shimmering barrier that acted as an invisible ceiling over the boats. Aeglors slammed directly into it and were stunned. Feathers flew. While they reeled, trying to reorient themselves, two terodax also smashed into the barrier.

"Ouch! Like birds hitting a window," Vic said.

On his massive sea serpent, King Barak shook his sea-urchin scepter. The merlon king reminded Vic of a capering chimpanzee, only much uglier and covered with scales.

Unharmed and dripping, Azric climbed onto his sea serpent's gleaming head, raised a hand into the air, and shouted. Answering his summons, a particularly large terodax swerved and dipped low to pluck Azric from the sea serpent and lift him into the air again.

The first few merlons climbed onto the deck of the war galley. Vic brought the carpet to land at the prow of the ship, so he, Lyssandra, and Tiaret could fight side by side to defend Ven Rubicas and the sages who were casting spells. Tiaret slammed a merlon on its tympanic membrane with the heavy end of her staff. The merlon stumbled back over the side and splashed into the water.

Continued explosions resounded in the sky. Standing near Ven Rubicas, Sage Snigmythya stumbled her way through a spell scroll and said "*S'ibah!*" A puff of greenish-black poison smoke appeared, spreading out in front of three aeglors, who flew directly into it, then reeled away, gasping and coughing. Obviously receiving a fatal dose of the poison, one turned gray and dropped like a stone into the water.

Though Rubicas's shield spell hovered up in the sky, the flying armies swiftly found ways around it and plunged down to the warships.

Vic, Tiaret, and Lyssandra kept fighting.

Sharif and Gwen sat on his carpet, defending one side of the *Bright Warrior* from attacking merlons.

With wind blowing in her face, Gwen shot her arrowpult and struck a merlon on its tympanic membrane. Howling and hissing, the scaled warrior slid back down into the ocean. Around them on the lead war galley, armed Elantyan soldiers slashed at the merlon attackers with swords.

With wind blowing in their faces at the war galley's prow, Virs Helassa and Parsimanias joined in reading intricate passages from a scroll to cast a hurricane spell. At the head of the flock of terodax, Azric was buffeted backward by the unexpected storm, but he drew the flying predators back together with magic and forced them onward.

Bradsinoreus shouted for his soldiers to stand firm and keep fighting. He was muscular and bearded, dressed in a crimson Elantyan cape and polished armor. Drumbeats urged the fighters to greater effort.

From her vantage point, Gwen saw a flash of thick, armored tentacles in the water below the galley. Something was down there—something much worse than the hideous sea serpents. In this incredible attack from both sea and sky, Barak commanded his huge force of merlons as Azric controlled the flying armies.

Admiral Bradsinoreus directed the defenders of Elantya, never shrinking from the two-pronged attack. The defense looked hopeless, even with the war galleys and the sages, but the commander remained strong. "We must hold them here at the crystal door!"

Gwen would not give up hope either.

Sharif moved the carpet closer to the hull and slashed at the stray merlons with his curved sword as they tried to climb onto the ship. He looked longingly at the open shimmering portal. Irrakesh was on the other side, along with all of his enslaved people. But though he was sultan of the flying city, Sharif had to deal with the greater danger, even though it pained him.

On a third war galley, Master Polup stood in his armored suit, clanking across the deck. The anemonite sage called for the oarsmen to turn the craft sideways, aiming the large cannon he'd installed.

Barak radiated confidence from his high sea serpent. With King Raathun and his aeglors, with the terodax, with his full merlon army, and with Azric commanding them all, Barak seemed much braver.

Gwen watched where the cannon was pointing.

With a loud *boom*, the cannon launched a large projectile that hit Barak's sea serpent squarely in the throat and killed it.

Although the explosion missed the merlon king, he fell backward off the sea monster with a roar of dismay and humiliation.

Sharif had a grim smile on his face. Elantyan soldiers cheered just as they had when seeing Azric knocked out of the sky. But Barak was not indestructible like the dark sage. The merlon king recovered, swam, and then dove beneath the waves as if to hide.

"That's got to hurt their morale," Gwen said.

Helassa and Parsimanias stood together chanting, raising their voices in perfect unison. The glowing aja letters on the scroll became bright and the winds picked up in a much greater storm than the bursts of wind they had previously created. The angry terodax back-flapped their wings, reminding Gwen of kites in a hurricane struggling to maintain their position, but the furious hurricane pushed them backward like an invisible hammer.

Clinging to his winged creature, Azric struggled in vain to keep the attack moving forward. His hair and robe fluttered backward as if they were about to be stripped away, and he barely kept his grip on the flying creature. He shouted, trying to form the words of a spell, but the sounds were snatched away in the roar. The flying army was being driven back!

Seeing the aeglors and terodax pushed toward the crystal door opening, Vic called to Sage Rubicas at the prow of the ship, "Can you move your shield, help push the aeglors and the terodax out of here? Use it like a battering ram to shove them back through the crystal door!"

The old man cracked his knuckles. "Of course, Viccus!"

Though the invisible shield wasn't large enough to cover the battleships in the Elantyan navy, it served well enough as a barricade, herding them along. The winds continued to shove the flying creatures back through the crystal door into the empty skies near Irrakesh.

"It is not enough just to push them through," Lyssandra said, kicking away a merlon. "We must close the door!"

The three friends looked with dismay at the crystal door leading to the barren deserts of Irrakesh. The sea serpent was still beached on the sand dunes on the other side of the portal, keeping the crystal door open. It lay gasping and covered with sand, obviously dying.

Suddenly, more merlons emerged in the water all around them, riding large whales that breached the surface. Tiaret pointed. "Ulbar!"

Vic whistled. "The cavalry has arrived!"

The rebel merlons clashed against the other aquatic warriors and splashing mayhem ensued. Ulbar guided his large black whale to where the sea serpent's tail hung in the water on their side of the crystal door. Another whale joined him, and the two opened their yawning mouths and bit down on the twitching snakelike tail without breaking the skin. They began to swim backward with all their strength. Though it was caught on the dry grasping sands, the sea serpent began to be dragged back into the water again.

Vic shouted to Tiaret. "Once they clear the doorway, slam it shut!"

The girl from Afirik was already standing at the prow of the ship, facing the door. The sea serpent left a long gouge in the sand dunes. It thrashed and twitched, but Vic figured it would welcome the possibility of being pulled back into the ocean.

The enormous windstorm created by the two Virs had pushed most of the aeglors and terodax back through into the other world. Though Azric struggled, wearing an expression of extreme vexation, he too succumbed and finally slipped backward through the crystal door.

Admiral Bradsinoreus called for the fighters on the decks of the war galleys to battle their opponents with renewed vigor.

King Barak rose from the water riding a powerful sea serpent beside Goldskin, his vicious female general. Snarling, he issued commands, and even Goldskin seemed afraid to see what the merlon leader was doing.

From Sharif's carpet above the *Bright Warrior*, Gwen saw something dark and dangerous rising through the water. One huge tentacle slipped above the waves, snapping like a whip. Spikes and beaten armor were strapped to the suckered appendage. Another tentacle rose, then another, until she lost count. An enormous bulbous head broke the surface like a swollen bag of wet leather. She had seen one of these horrible creatures before.

A battle kraken.

This one, unlike the one that had caused so much havoc in the Elantyan harbor, was riderless and guided directly by merlon commands. In one swift action, all of the tentacles wrapped around the *Bright Warrior*. Vir Helassa tried to shout a spell, while Parsimanias ducked.

"Watch out!" Sharif said, knocking Gwen to the carpet as a huge terodax swept past, raking at them with its talons. They shot at the creature with their arrowpults until, injured, it retreated. Fortunately, neither of the friends got more than a few scratches.

Below, like thrashing snakes, the tentacles snatched the mast and snapped it, bringing the heavy wooden pole down with a crash that splintered the rails.

Admiral Bradsinoreus stood on the aftcastle, bellowing orders to the archers and spearmen. Elantyans peppered the monster with long bronze-tipped spears and sharp arrows—to no effect.

The storm winds began to falter as Helassa and Parsimanias tried to call upon a new defensive spell. Parsimanias screamed and grabbed the statuesque woman's red sleeve as a gigantic tentacle crashed down upon them. The battle kraken's blow shattered the prow of the war galley, crushing the two Virs.

Gwen could not believe what she had just seen. Two of the five members of the Pentumvirate were now dead!

The soldiers threw long harpoons and jagged spears, trying to do anything possible to drive away the gigantic undersea creature. Then more tentacles wrapped around the war galley like monstrously powerful pythons.

Gwen and Sharif might well be next. A tentacle quested upward toward his flying carpet. They shot at it, to no apparent effect.

Bradsinoreus took a harpoon himself, bent over the side of the wrecked galley, and hurled the thick spear into the soft, fleshy head of the sea monster. In reflex, one of the kraken's tentacles twitched sideways and struck the military leader a blow powerful enough to smash his ribs and knock him overboard as easily as a maid sweeping up a bit of dust.

Sharif circled his carpet around the kraken and back toward the ship, but before the two could get there, the battle kraken completely crushed the war galley, splintering the long wooden keel and pulling the debris down into the churning water. Its tentacles wrapped around the galley and snapped the huge ship like a handful of twigs. Pieces flew in all directions. Oars shattered.

"We've got to help!" Gwen said, and Sharif took the carpet down and hovered it just above the water. They both caught a quick breath before plunging into the sea. The impact of the water made Gwen reel, and with a familiar choking inhalation, she filled her lungs with water and forced herself to breathe through her gill slits.

Sharif, too, adapted to the water breathing, and the two of them swam downward, away from the giant tentacled monster. Sharp wooden shards from the wreckage swirled around them like floating daggers. Gwen and Sharif dodged the dangerous debris, swimming away from the sinking ship. She gestured wildly underwater, searching for any survivors.

Amongst the wreckage and the bodies of fallen soldiers, they encountered the drifting Admiral Bradsinoreus. Blood streamed from his mouth and from wounds in his sides, yet he still struggled feebly ... and he was drowning.

Gwen and Sharif worked together to grab the man, stroking evenly to bring him to the surface. Pulling the military leader's head out of the water, Gwen heard him cough and choke. "We'll get you to safety," she said.

"My ship! My soldiers ..."

But he was in no condition to struggle.

While the battle kraken ripped apart what remained of the lead war galley, Gwen and Sharif pulled the admiral up onto the carpet. From above, she could hear Vic's voice yelling wildly for her.

With the sinking of the lead war galley and the death of the two Virs, a pall of shock seemed to hang over the watery battlefield.

Ulbar and his rebels finally succeeded in yanking the sea serpent free of the sand dunes, pulling it back to the ocean side of the crystal door. Ulbar hissed something in merlon.

Vic cried out, watching Gwen and Sharif approach with the injured Bradsinoreus. "The crystal door, Tiaret."

Now that the magical winds had faded with the loss of

Helassa and Parsimanias, a handful of terodax and aeglors from Azric's flying army flew back through the door with renewed confidence.

There was a mere fraction of a second between a pair of aeglors when nothing was passing through the sparkling gateway—but it was enough for Tiaret.

She slammed the crystal door shut, leaving Azric and the rest of his army trapped with Irrakesh, just as she had done when the apprentices had escaped from the flying city.

Vic felt sickened. "They'll just break through again. There are lots of Keys in Irrakesh. They found a way to open it in the first place."

Gwen and Sharif, with Bradsinoreus, landed on the deck of the *Thunder Shield*. Healers rushed to the wounded admiral.

Something fell into place in Sharif's mind. A moment after watching Tiaret slam shut the crystal door on Azric and his flying armies, Sharif understood that he could seal this crystal door forever. *No one* would be able to break through. He also knew that his action would trap his people in Irrakesh. Still, he did what he had to do.

Sharif raised his hands and "traced" the opening in the air. Crackling lines like orange embroidery delineated the crystal doorway. He sketched the outline again and again with his hands. Finally, the fiery lines faded, and the door was sealed. Sharif's legs gave way beneath him, and he fell to the deck.

"Did you just do what I think you did?" Vic asked.

Sharif nodded. "It is sealed."

"That is an important power," Lyssandra said, offering her vial of greenstepe to Tiaret and Sharif.

While Sharif took a few gulps, Vic tried to console the other young man. "I can still tear open a new portal when the time is right."

Tiaret said, "At the moment we still have merlons to contend with. Look!" The battle kraken, as if unsatisfied with its attack, continued to smash the debris of the already destroyed war galley.

Though King Barak still had the tentacled monster under his control, his main force of merlons was now engaged in a fight against Ulbar's rebels as well. Master Polup's cannon blasted again, and this time the projectile pummeled the enormous battle kraken.

Ulbar and several of his rebel merlons drove their whales and orcas, ramming the tentacled sea beast. Barak, riding beside Goldskin, snarled again and, not wanting to continue this battle alone, sounded a retreat.

The battle kraken submerged, severely wounded. The sea serpents slashed and snapped several of the rebel merlons, but then they all dove, fleeing from a battle that had turned against them. Even though they had won for now, Vic did not feel at all like celebrating.

CHAPTER 26

I t was a cheerless battle fleet that limped back toward the harbor in Elantya. Red alarm pennants fluttered from every mast. Vic was in shock, as were the other members of the Ring of Might. He had not been surprised by the strength or viciousness of the attack by Azric's combined forces, but he had not expected the deaths of Helassa and Parsimanias. Admiral Bradsinoreus, still unconscious, lay below decks under the watchful care of Lyssandra's mother, Kaisa. The pitiful few other survivors from the destroyed ship were still being treated by healers.

Vic tried to comfort Tiaret who, despite her stoic nature, had been hardest hit of them all. The girl from Afirik had both admired and understood Helassa, and a mutual respect had grown between the two fighting women.

Vic wasn't quite sure why he did it—it wasn't as if he was in charge of anything—but he went to Ven Sage Rubicas and said, "We've, uh, got a bit of a break right now with Azric sealed up in Irrakesh, and everyone in the fleet is hurting from all our losses. They know they'll have to fight again sometime soon, so I'd like to hold a short memorial on the main deck. I think it'll help us start healing."

To his surprise, the Ven Sage did not offer to lead the memorial or to take charge of the event. He simply said, "I will attend."

So Vic and Gwen called most of the people on the *Thunder Shield* to the deck and lit the brazier to signify a time to share. Tiaret was the first to stand and speak. "Helassa is no longer with us. Her name is already honored in the Great Epic and shall be again."

A smattering of muffled sobs came from the crowd. Tiaret drew herself up straight and proud. "But she would not wish us to weep for her. Helassa's spirit was made of fire and xyridium. In the face of danger, she did not waver. She did not retreat. She did not break. She told me once that from the first day she became the Vir of Protection, she was ready to give up her life to block the spread of evil through the crystal doors. She had no doubt this day would come. Helassa is dead," she said bluntly, "but the fire of her spirit is not extinguished so long as it burns in me and in every one of us who refuse to allow evil to have its way. Do not spend your tears for her—or even for yourselves."

Vic smiled listening to his friend. He had expected a somber, mournful event. Instead, the energizing effect, as Tiaret's clear voice carried to the crowd, was already obvious.

"Celebrate the life of our Vir of Protection. Fuel the fire of Helassa in your hearts. There let it blaze and burn away all discouragement and weariness, self-pity, anxiety, insecurity, or any thought for yourself beyond this: that we will never surrender, that we must stand in the way of evil wherever we find it until Elantya and Irrakesh and the other worlds through the crystal doors are safe once more."

The ceremony continued for another hour as, one after

another, people came forward to share uplifting memories of Vir Helassa, Vir Parsimanias, and the many others who had perished with them.

Sea birds cried and circled overhead as the ships pulled into Elantya's harbor.

CHAPTER 27

Gwen had hoped they would have more time to recover from the disastrous sea battle at the crystal door. Far sooner than they had ever expected, the war began again.

It was bright noon, and to all appearances, the day was cheerful. The seas were calm. Galleys patrolled the harbor and coastline. Guards stood watch in high towers, ready to signal with quicksilver mirrors and wind crystals. The entire city waited for the next threat, although with the crystal door to Irrakesh sealed, they were sure they had hobbled the dark sage for the time being. King Barak showed little inclination to fight this war all on his own.

Gwen and Vic, with Dr. Pierce and their friends, were eating lunch together when Sharif brought his flying carpet in to hover a few feet off the ground in front of them. "I have just made another circuit. Everything is quiet."

"Too quiet," Tiaret said. "I do not trust this peace. It unnerves me."

Vic chuckled nervously. "Battling merlons and pterodactyl men unnerves me."

"And seeing people get hurt," Gwen added. Hoping to find out what Azric was planning, she had opened several windows. But after witnessing repeated scenes of torture of the citizens of Irrakesh—without learning anything helpful—she had decided to rest a while before trying again.

"I do not like this waiting," Lyssandra said. "I continue to dream of things that may happen. One thing I am sure of: we must combine our powers in new ways if we hope to save Elantya, Szishh, and Irrakesh. That time is soon—today, I believe."

A flock of birds whipped around the buildings nearby, cawing at each other, then winging away. Gwen started instinctively at the sound, but these were birds that lived on the island, not attacking aeglors. She looked up to watch the white-winged birds flying around, chasing insects, then spreading apart. In the sky above Elantya, a network of white cracks appeared, as if someone had spun a spider web in emptiness. The air split like a breaking mirror, then opened, spreading wide. Gwen felt a deep chill.

"A new crystal door!" Lyssandra cried.

"No," Vic said. "The one I created. I thought it was gone."

"I shut it, but it apparently still functions," Tiaret said.

Sharif said, "I did not seal that door because I did not yet know my power. The winged soldiers who saw us escape must have told Azric it was there."

"All Azric needed was a Master Key, and he already had the only one in Irrakesh," Gwen said. "Jabir."

Dr. Pierce sounded the alarm. The people of Elantya responded quickly. Watchtower sentries transmitted warning flashes. Armored guards and citizens ran out of their buildings, took whatever weapons they had gathered for this situation, and raced to positions they had been assigned during various drills.

"You kids do what you need to do," Uncle Cap said. "I've got to supervise our defenses on the harbor cliffs." Giving Vic and Gwen each a hug, he rushed out.

The crystal door opened wider and wider. Gwen leaned backward. Her mouth dropped open as she stared at the gigantic object coming through. Because Irrakesh was as large as the island of Elantya, it seemed to move very slowly. Yet Gwen knew how swiftly Azric must be driving it. As the city pushed through Vic's new crystal door, the boundaries widened to accommodate its passage. Irrakesh hung like an enormous mountain overhead.

A heavy shadow fell across all of Elantya. Gwen knew that even if Ven Rubicas used all of his remaining spell scrolls to create a protective barrier, he couldn't form a shield wide enough to stop the floating city.

Gwen quickly opened a small window onto the city. They all stared at it. The enormous central Palace of Irrakesh had many balconies and openings. Azric was using the one outside the throne room as a command platform from which to guide this overwhelming attack. He held Vizier Jabir. The wizard looked even more battered, bruised, and bloodied than before, and Gwen knew that Azric or King Raathun had tortured the vizier further, and perhaps his family, until he had opened the new crystal door to Elantya.

Now that the flying city was partway through the portal, aeglors flew up from their perches, leaving the towers and minarets and rooftops, swarming forward in another army. Their numbers seemed far greater than any Gwen had ever seen before. She supposed that Azric, while licking his wounds from his defeat out in the ocean, had gathered reinforcements from the floating kelptree forests where Raathun ruled the aeglors. He must have drawn all the population of the winged men. The terodax numbers seemed infinite as well. This was indeed the final battle, Gwen could see. Azric would have drawn all of his slaves, all of the terodax and the aeglors. He might even have broken the wills of some of the people of Irrakesh. He would not risk failure again.

But before the city had passed completely through the crystal door, it paused its forward motion and floated in place, forcing the crystal door to remain open so that Azric and all his armies could pass back and forth at will. Azric stood on the balcony working his own ancient magic. Mist rose from the water, congealing into swirling clouds, swelling and shifting, not dissipated by the sea breezes.

"There is something familiar in this," Lyssandra said.

"He's just grandstanding," Vic said.

The cloud of mist altered its shape until it formed the enormous form of the dark sage Azric. The blue and green eyes in his ageless misty face glowed as it loomed high above Elantya, larger than several buildings stacked on top of each other. His expression was benevolent, almost kind.

"He looks like an Air Spirit," Sharif said as Gwen let her window fall shut.

Azric spoke, his smooth voice once again magically amplified. "Surrender now and become my loyal subjects. Throwing away your lives will serve no purpose. Take this opportunity to save yourselves. I assure you, I would prefer to show you mercy; I truly would." The voice grew harsh now. "But if you deny me, your lives are forfeit. The consequences will be unavoidable."

As the dark sage's voice boomed out, Lyssandra grew pale, and her cobalt eyes went wide. "I saw this in a dream—Azric's giant form looming over the city."

"At least you know what it means now," Vic said. "He's just a big bag of wind—no substance."

"A windbag with a huge army," Gwen said.

From the cliffs near the harbor, cannons fired at the dark sage's image.

"Fools!" Azric roared. The gigantic misty face became a thundercloud. Then like a plague of giant locusts, the terodax and the aeglors poured downward onto Elantya.

CHAPTER 28

While the city of Irrakesh loomed ominously over the island and Azric's threatening declaration still resounded in the air, another attack came from the sea. Elantyans scrambled for their final defenses, and the Ring of Might gathered the weapons they had chosen—clubs, arrowpults, sunshine bombs made from collected mirror mill energy, crystal daggers, and of course Sharif's curved sword and Tiaret's teaching staff. Again the friends split up on the two flying carpets. Sharif and Gwen sped toward the harbor where the war galleys were about to launch. Vic, Lyssandra, and Tiaret raced away as well. The five of them would use their powers and their imaginations to assist in the fight. All of Elantya had to pull together now.

The merlons rose up, King Barak and his female general Goldskin riding enormous armored sea serpents. Merlon warriors swam in the waves, ready to storm the beaches and the docks. Thousands of branded sharks raced forward, their sharp teeth open in wide jaws. And this time Barak had brought other monstrous creatures from the darkest depths of the sea, lifting them up from the deep trenches and controlling them with water magic.

Gwen saw not only the deadly battle kraken that had destroyed the war galley and killed the two Virs, but two more. In their first attack on Elantya, not long after Vic and Gwen had stumbled into this world from Earth, a single battle kraken had wrought terrible damage on the island, sinking innumerable ships out in the deep waters at the edge of the harbor. This time, faced with so many sea serpents, three battle krakens, and a force of merlon warriors three times what they had seen before, Gwen knew Elantya was in for a difficult battle.

And that wasn't even factoring in whatever destruction Azric and the flying warriors could rain down on them from the skies.

"Where should we start?" Gwen asked Sharif.

He took the carpet out to the waiting warships. "We can fight and face them over water."

"Sure," Gwen agreed, though she was tense. She glanced down. "We've already been under the water and faced a battle kraken. How much worse can it get?"

"I can think of many ways," Sharif said, but she didn't ask him to elaborate.

Vir Questas was on the *Thunder Shield* waiting to be dispatched. Sharif and Gwen offered to fly above them, help with defense, and be their lookouts. With Virs Helassa and Parsimanias both dead and Admiral Bradsinoreus severely wounded and unable to direct the battle, the remaining Virs and Elantyan sages had to do it all. The Vir of Learning's warm eyes looked sad and troubled after all he had recently endured. "I will accept any assistance in this fight, and while I know Vir Parsimanias was skeptical, I have seen the apprentices of Ven Rubicas demonstrate enough amazing abilities that I would never underestimate you."

"We won't let you down," Gwen said.

With a burst of speed and strength, the war galley raced away from the docks, its sharp prow cutting the water, heading out to where King Barak's undersea armies were ready to launch their major attack.

On three small ships that headed out to the mouth of the harbor, Ven Sage Rubicas, Vir Etherya, and Sage Abacas read from spell scrolls and cast the invisible barricade spells, setting up shimmering blockades that covered most of the water, but they did not have the power or breadth to block the entire passage. Still, it created a bottleneck, and as the merlons and their captive sea monsters rushed forward, they crashed into the invisible blockade and were forced to swim around. This delayed them, but not for long enough.

With Vir Questas in command, Sharif and Gwen guiding them from above, and an Elantyan captain pushing the *Thunder Shield* forward, they soon got close enough to see the merlons. More dark and ugly forms rose up from the depths, plunging toward them.

"It appears that King Barak saved some surprises for this attack," Sharif said.

Besides the three enormous armored battle krakens and the dozen huge sea serpents that raced forward, three long-necked dinosaur-like creatures also reared their sinuous heads above the waves, flashing bright red eyes in the sunlight. They opened their mouths and snapped. Gwen thought they looked like the Loch Ness monster or the prehistoric creatures called plesiosaurs; all were denizens of the darkest depths.

Amongst all of the triangular shark fins, another dorsal projection cut the water, rising upward and curving, leopard-spotted on gray skin. This behemoth shark must have been ten times the size of the largest whale shark on Earth. Far from being a peaceful plankton-eating fish like the whale sharks

Gwen had studied in marine biology, this creature had tooth-filled jaws wide enough to swallow a small boat.

"Do all creatures from the deep waters need such large teeth?" Sharif wondered aloud. He and Gwen took turns shouting descriptions down to Vir Questas.

The ships blasted with their cannons, throwing blazing balls of powerful Grogyptian Fire at the largest targets. One blast struck the behemoth shark, which submerged quickly, possibly injured, but because of the magic in the merlon brands on its hide, it was forced to continue fighting. Sea serpents rammed the outermost war galleys, and though sages cast warding spells and Elantyan soldiers threw harpoons and shot arrows to drive back the beasts, the aquatic armies inflicted a great deal of damage. Gwen lobbed a sunshine bomb.

One of the battle krakens intentionally struck out toward a small boat holding a sage who had cast one of the shield spells. The panicked sage abandoned his ship before the tentacles could grasp him. His spell faltered and a section of the shimmering barricade faded away. On the *Thunder Shield*, Vir Questas pulled out spell scrolls. Sharif and Gwen swooped down, and each took several, ready to do their part to fight.

Before they could reach the main mass of merlon soldiers and the towering sea serpent ridden by Goldskin, who carried a sharp trident spear, the water around the ship began to bubble and boil. Small fish with sharp fins that acted as wings emerged. Their large eyes saw food in every object, and sharp, needlelike teeth could tear wood and cloth and flesh. Hundreds of the creatures sprang out of the water and flung themselves like gnawing locusts onto the war galley.

"Flying piranhas!" Gwen cried.

Sharif was grim. "They almost killed us last time."

The soldiers on deck shouted and ran for weapons. The ravenous fish began to chew and splinter the hull, the railings, the mast. The rowers could barely lift their oars. Each one had five or six flying piranhas fastened to them, snapping away the sleek, curved edges. Other flying piranhas devoured the rudder. More attacked the sails.

Sharif and Gwen rapidly read all of the protective spell scrolls they had, driving away flying piranhas by the dozens, stunning them, forcing them away from the war galley. Others lay flopping on the deck, and they shot them with their arrow-pults, though the hand weapons seemed woefully inadequate against so many. The flying piranhas were not King Barak's primary attack, but they certainly preoccupied Vir Questas's warship.

The sea serpents surged forward. Goldskin raised her trident and let out a loud battle cry. King Barak on his sea serpent shouted frantically, already declaring his ultimate victory. The aeglors and terodax had begun their full-fledged strike on Elantya. They had gone inland and were damaging the towers, the rooftops, and streets, chasing people who fought back with spears, arrows, torches, and household spells.

Gwen hoped her cousin and friends on the other flying carpet were still all right and causing great damage. Right now, though, she had her hands full as a hundred more flying piranhas rose from the sea and began to rip the sails to shreds. Some went after the flying carpet, and several of the dangerous fish had fastened themselves to her sleeves and the back of her blouse. She and Sharif used the heavy clubs they had brought to knock them off.

Having gone around the invisible barricades, many of the sea serpents and the three battle krakens plunged toward the inner harbor. Gwen knew that once they reached the docks and the shore, they would cause unimaginable damage.

Then more merlon soldiers surged forward and began scram-bling up the hulls of other warships, fighting the Elantyan soldiers hand-to-hand in a clash of sharp weapons. Gwen couldn't imagine how the island, even with all its sages, weapons, and ingenuity, could possibly stand against this. Colorful sky fireworks exploded, erupting in flashes of sparks and smoke up in the air. Additional booms occurred underwater, driving some of the undersea attackers back. Sharif landed the carpet on the deck, and Gwen knocked a pair of flying piranhas away from Vir Questas as he finished reading a protective spell that made himself, Gwen, and Sharif invisible to the ravenous fish.

"Gwenya, I have something I must do, and I must go alone," Sharif said, whacking a piranha that flopped on the deck.

Gwen shook her head. "I'll go with you."

"No. It is a danger I must face, and you will be safer here with Vir Questas." Before Gwen could object again, Sharif put his carpet into a steep climb and was gone.

The battle became infinitely worse.

At the mouth of the harbor, dark shapes erupted from the surface. Long, wooden masts appeared, covered with rotted and waterlogged sails. Huge, algae-covered wrecks, now studded with barnacles and shells, were crewed by gasping merlons who looked like drowned sailors on the decks of ghost ships. These twenty-five vessels had sunk and been left at the bottom of the ocean, rotting hulks of once proud sailing vessels. Now, through some unknown merlon magic, they were all brought to the surface.

Though it didn't seem possible that they could even float, the once-sunken wrecks now drove forward, the first ones ramming an Elantyan war galley. Two others turned strange coral-encrusted gun ports toward the island and, with loud explosions, blasted out glossy golden projectiles that seemed to shimmer with internal heat.

"This is water magic," Vir Questas said.

As the projectiles struck buildings and wharves in Elantya, brilliant silvery explosions sent out shock waves of magic, igniting devastating fires that charred wood and raced up the stone walls, causing them to crumble.

"Lavaja bombs," Gwen said in shock.

"Ah," Vir Questas said. "We knew the merlons had thousands of them. We found all of the ones planted beneath Elantya, but the merlons must have kept stockpiles."

The wrecked ships launched volley after volley of the lavaja missiles. The detonations were far more powerful than the blasts from Sage Polup's improved Grogyptian Fire cannons. Behind the rotting hulks of vessels that continued to plunge forward, a last sunken ship rose up. Gwen recognized it even before it had finished emerging into the air. Water streamed off its battered hull, splintered sides, and broken masts. The shape was very familiar, though. She would recognize the *Golden Walrus* anywhere.

At its prow stood a pale-skinned human form whose features looked distressingly *wrong*. The man's skin seemed to be made of melting wax. His eyes were uneven and boiling with fury. A few patches of dark hair stuck to the scalp, though the rest of his head was one gigantic scar. Some of the fingers on his hand were fused together, but not webbed like the merlons'. No, this man was damaged but alive. He was also ruthless, powerful, and ready for revenge.

Gwen was unwilling to admit what she knew in her dread-filled heart.

"The spy Orpheon," Vir Questas said. "The former apprentice of the Ven Sage."

"I watched him fall into the lavaja and burn," Gwen said.

"But he is immortal, like Azric. Though the magic in the lavaja seems to have injured him, he cannot be killed by normal means. He is alive and has come to fight us."

"As if we needed another enemy right now," Gwen said in dismay.

From the *Walrus*, Orpheon shouted out orders. "Obliterate Elantya. Wipe out the sages. Annihilate them all!"

The *Golden Walrus* was also equipped with the new merlon coral-tube cannons. More lavaja bombs blasted out, raining down on the beautiful buildings of Elantya. Loud thunderclaps came from overhead. Striking a pair of flying piranhas, Gwen looked upward to see another terrible magical storm brewing.

CHAPTER 29

Racing up toward Irrakesh on his flying carpet, Sharif felt vulnerable. As the future sultan, he could not drive back his dismay at knowing that he had let his people down. His entire city had been enslaved by the aeglors and terodax. Now that most of the winged warriors were away attacking Elantya, Sharif used the situation to his advantage. If he could get to his people and make them listen, perhaps they would fight back.

Although the force of merlons, aeglors, and terodax was formidable, the people of Irrakesh could join the battle. He clung to a grim determination that he could indeed do something unexpected that would help to defeat Azric. He would do this for his father and for Hashim and for all those who had lost something to the terrible dark sage.

He also hoped to find a chance to free Piri. He could not stand the thought that Azric had captured her and was forcing her to do his bidding.

His carpet streaked upward. Instead of fighting any enemies

he encountered, he dodged and outran them. His carpet was extremely swift, and he was going in the opposite direction from the terodax and aeglors. Irrakesh, full of people—*his* people— still hung halfway through the open crystal door, a gigantic living doorstop. As Sharif approached the familiar buildings, he noticed that the pennants were now frayed, awnings torn, marketplace shut down, and citizens trapped inside their homes.

Clouds had begun to grow thicker. Lightning flashed. This was no natural storm. Seeing Azric on the high balcony of the palace, watching the battle, ready to take over, Sharif guessed that Piri must be with him somewhere close. He raced forward, his hair crackling with static electricity.

Lightning bolts skittered across the sky, and when Azric glanced about uneasily, Sharif realized with a start that the dark sage's magic was not producing the lightning. *He* had not summoned the storm. This new development was not part of Azric's battle plan.

Lights coalesced into sparkling forms that seemed to fill the air—shimmering shapes not unlike the misty visage that Azric had projected on the clouds. Sharif's heart swelled. He had seen such shapes before and suspected their origin. At last!

Azric drew glowing runes in the air to cast spells, calling up wind, sending loud thunderclaps out at the bright lights. The dark sage seemed distinctly uneasy. Determined, Sharif raced toward the palace balcony. The massive, powerful forms took more distinct shapes in the clouds, a looming man and woman in exotic simulated garb. Their angry faces glowered down at Azric.

Many powerful figures took shape in the air, scowling at the great palace and the small-looking dark sage who opposed them. Sharif could understand now the awe and mystery that had caused the people of Irrakesh to name these powerful beings Air Spirits. Because Azric had imprisoned several of their kind in ages past and had now enslaved Piri, the djinni had come to exact revenge and rescue her.

Azric's attention was entirely focused on the attacking Air Spirits. Hundreds of aeglors and terodax looped back around toward Irrakesh. Almost as a casual gesture, the djinnis swept their incorporeal hands sideways and blasted large numbers of the winged warrior army out of the skies, smashing wings, singeing feathers, and sending the dark sage's allies plummeting to their deaths. The cloudy figures converged on Azric.

Sharif plunged forward like a projectile with a predetermined target. So focused was Azric on trying to drive the angry djinnis back, that he didn't notice Sharif until the last moment. The dark sage turned, his expression filled with alarm and disbelief to see the purple carpet racing toward him. Sharif braced for impact. Azric tried to defend himself, but the carpet bowled him over and sent the dark sage sprawling on the ornately tiled balcony.

Holding tightly to his purple rug, Sharif soared upward again until he caught sight of the object he was looking for: an amber and purple bottle with a bulbous base. Since capturing her, Azric had kept Piri in the glowing jeweled container, asking her questions and draining her life force. Sharif knew no magic to get her out, but he could save her from Azric.

While Azric scrambled to his feet, Sharif swooped down, snatched up the bottle, and laughed with delight. The dark sage no doubt would have continued asking Piri questions that would help him destroy Elantya. Not only would Piri have been tortured by the thought of harming all those people, Sharif knew she would not have lived much longer. Holding the bottle by its neck, he sailed up into the air as the ominous, shimmering Air Spirits continued their thunderous attack, buffeting the floating city as if it were a rowboat in a typhoon.

"Here!" Sharif shouted to the closest Air Spirits. "I have Piri.

Can you free her?" He grasped the long neck of the ornate bottle and with all his strength flung it out into the sky. The Air Spirits clustered around it like gathering clouds. Bright lights flashed and they dissolved the bottle entirely, breaking the spell, disintegrating the barriers that held Piri trapped.

She seemed to explode into the small but perfect form of a glowing, dazzling young lady—but much more than that. She spread her arms wide, her long hair fluttering behind her like silk in a windstorm, and launched herself up into the air. Sharif could not stop grinning. His heart was filled with joy. He threw open his arms and called, "You are free, Piri."

The Air Spirits boomed. "Come, Piri. You are safe now. We must take you home."

She shook her head. *I refuse.*

"We can better guard you there."

You did not, Piri pointed out. *Safe with Sharif.*

"Come with us. They drain our power. This is not our war."

Safe with Sharif, she insisted. *His war, my war.*

"Do you invoke the Ancient Magic, then?" one of the Air Spirits asked.

Sharif friend. Piri flew to his side. *Stay with friend.*

"If it is your wish," another looming djinni said, "then it is your right. Draw on the Ancient Magic, Young One."

As Sharif raced away from Irrakesh on his carpet, Piri, no larger than his forearm, dove and looped and twirled along beside him.

Though the aeglors did not engage the enormous Air Spirits, the terodax were less intelligent. Dozens of them swooped toward the djinni and were immediately blasted out of the air. With lightning cracks and a roar of gale-force breezes, the Air Spirits flooded back through the crystal door into the skies above Irrakesh and dissipated.

But Piri stayed. Piri was free. How could Sharif have hoped for anything better? Tears of gratitude welled up in his eyes, but he knew his work was not done. Elantya and Irrakesh both needed him. Together he and Piri turned their efforts toward the continuing battle.

CHAPTER 30

When Tiaret crouched on the large flying carpet holding her teaching staff, Vic thought she looked like a lioness poised to protect her cubs. Even Lyssandra, sitting at the back of the carpet, looked formidable. Vic took the carpet low to the water. Upon seeing Tiaret, he was sure the merlons would turn around and flee rather than face her fury—if they had any sense. On the other hand, he didn't think that Barak's merlons had any sense.

The aquatic warriors were swimming through the waters toward the city. Up in the sky, aeglors and terodax continued their major attack, and if the merlon warriors reached the shore, they would swarm through the streets, intent on destroying everything they found.

"I am ready for them, friend Viccus," Tiaret said.

"I am not so certain," Lyssandra said.

Holding a club in one hand and flying the carpet with the other, Vic shrugged. "Fight now, agonize later, right?" He headed toward the hissing, scaly merlons. "I've bashed plenty of merlons in my day," he said. "I can do that. It's all those other things out there that worry me."

From the edge of the harbor, the three battle krakens and the line of powerfully armored sea serpents were making a great froth in the water as they charged toward the docks. Goldskin and King Barak held back, guiding their troops, letting the first waves of attacking monsters form a shock front to weaken the Elantyan resistance.

Once again, Ulbar and his rebel merlons arrived to join the battle. Ulbar and his merlons rose up with a mighty roar. Many were mounted on orcas and whales, while others clutched the dorsal fins of dolphins. They rode in among Barak's warriors, causing absolute mayhem.

"Barak will not retreat easily this time," Tiaret predicted.

"Some people just never learn their lesson," Vic said.

They reached the first line of merlon soldiers that were heading toward the beach. With a yowl of defiance, Tiaret attacked, leaning out over the water and swinging her teaching staff. They raised their sea-urchin clubs and their scalloped-edged swords and clashed them against her blur of a teaching staff. Lyssandra picked off merlons with her arrowpult in her right hand and a spear in her left. Vic joined in the battle. With a heavy club, he smacked a merlon on the forehead, causing its tympanic membranes to ring with pain.

Elantyans ran along the shore with weapons, forming a line to block the merlon advance as some of the sea people made it to the beach.

"It cannot be," Lyssandra said, pointing toward the edge of the harbor, where several ghost ships were visible. "The *Golden Walrus!*"

Vic smacked another merlon and looked up. As they watched, two Elantyan war galleys charged, the sailors rowing swiftly. Magically enhanced breezes caught their sails and pushed them forward.

Vic was shocked to see the sharpened prow of the lead galley —the one that Gwen and Sharif had been helping—plow directly into the rotted hull of one of the recently surfaced ghost ships. Wood cracked, hulls splintered, but the armored prow of the *Thunder Shield* was stronger. The keel of the ghost ship broke, and its already rotted and mangled framework began to fall apart.

Ulbar's rebels surged in to attack the sea monsters, and five more rebel merlons, including Ulbar himself, rose out of the water riding giant broad-winged jhantas, like the huge manta creature that Sharif had befriended in the merlon city. Throwing spears and hurling spiked balls, the merlon rebels on the jhantas concentrated their assault on the behemoth shark that had already been wounded by a blast of Grogyptian Fire. By now, however, the worse monsters had almost reached the main wharf.

The sea serpents and battle krakens would overpower Elantya's defenses. Vic could see the impending disaster. Everything would change within a few moments. Suddenly he had an idea. Tiaret bashed an oncoming merlon soldier, twirled her teaching staff, and stabbed another sea warrior that tried to attack an Elantyan citizen.

"Tiaret, I need your help," Vic said. "Why fight a couple of merlons when we can defeat all of the battle krakens and several sea serpents if we work together?"

Tiaret stopped. "Yes. That would be preferable. But how?"

"I'll do my thing, and you do yours. The five of us have special powers for a reason, you know. Lyssandra, we'll need you to cover us while we concentrate. Remember, you said we needed to learn new ways to combine our powers."

Waving tentacles in the air, the three battle krakens swam

forward, their bodies like bloated spiders, their round yellow eyes enormous and implacable. The sea serpents thrashed and hissed. Their spiny fins looked threatening. The patterns of leopard spots on their scales made them appear even more dangerous. Merlon commanders rode on some of them, while others simply plowed forward like destructive machines.

"We can stop them from getting to the wharf—I think." Vic held out his hands, drew a deep breath, and thought about how he had worked his personal magic several times. It had been easy and instinctive.

A terodax dove toward them, rattling Vic's concentration.

"Focus!" Lyssandra said. She pitched a sunshine bomb at the terodax, striking it at the juncture of its body and wing and blowing the creature to bits.

In his mind, Vic sketched an imaginary boundary in the air and, exactly as he had hoped, a large crystalline arch appeared, like a mirror that cracked and broke—a new crystal door leading to a strange and possibly unexplored place. Did he dare unleash these monsters on some unsuspecting world? Vic wondered. Gwen could always check in on them later to make sure they weren't wreaking havoc in their new home, he supposed. *Big picture now, fine-tune later*, he told himself. The crystal door opened wide just in front of the charging battle krakens and the sea serpents.

Before they could stop or change their course, the monsters plunged through the crystal door and vanished. Right now, they were arriving on another world without merlons or slave masters to force them into causing destruction. Who knew? Maybe they would be happy there.

With a bright, hard-edged grin on her face, Tiaret summoned the magic within herself to slam the crystal door shut. One moment it sparkled in the air, the next it was gone. And the most gigantic and powerful monsters in the enemy navy had simply vanished from the battlefield. "An excellent idea, Viccus."

Screaming in fury from his sea serpent, King Barak seemed suddenly and desperately weak. Beside him, Goldskin looked uneasy. She waved her trident in the air and commanded the merlons to continue fighting.

From the battered *Golden Walrus*, Orpheon launched several more lavaja bombs. One exploded on the shore behind the carpet. Rocks and sand sprayed up from the blast, and Vic turned to look at Azric's henchman. An Elantyan war galley rammed a second ghost ship, smashing it and sinking it for good this time. The battle was far from hopeless. Vic flew the carpet toward the shore, where a line of merlons was emerging from the waves. Though more and more of them got past the island's defenses and up onto the beach, the Elantyan citizens fought to drive them back and Tiaret threw herself into the fray. Vic could see that the odds were improving.

CHAPTER 31

The skies cleared when the djinnis departed, carrying the storm and discharges with them. But the air over Elantya was still crowded with terodax and aeglors. Their squawking, hissing, and shrieking made a deafening clamor in Sharif's ears.

From the battlements on the distant cliffs of the island, Sage Pierce's newly emplaced cannons blasted up at the airborne warriors, scattering flocks of terodax, killing numerous aeglors. Unfortunately, some of the Grogyptian Fire blasted craters into the underbelly of the flying city, as well. The rock foundation of Irrakesh began to crumble and boulders rained down from above. The cannons continued to rumble, desperately defending the island.

Sharif couldn't let his beloved city fall apart, even if Azric was still in control of it. He traced some aja threads in his carpet pattern, and the rug headed back up to Irrakesh. Piri streaked ahead of Sharif, a glowing feminine ball of energy that flowed and flitted, scattering aeglors and producing showers of brown feathers. Azric had climbed to his feet on the balcony. Sharif wished the Air Spirits had swept the dark sage away with them, keeping him prisoner in the clouds as Azric had imprisoned Piri in a bottle.

Circling to the other side of the city, Sharif flew low and shouted down into the streets. "This is your prince, people of Irrakesh. The aeglors are battling Elantya. You must help. This is the time to rise up. Break away from your guards—they are few and you are many. You must join this fight *now*, for as our people say, 'Only the fool delays what must be done.'" He cruised lower, repeating his command in a loud voice, and people ventured forth from their homes and shelters. Piri flitted along with him, shining like a small sun.

Only a handful of aeglors remained in the city. Most of them had taken wing from the rooftops to dive down into the battle. "Spread the word. Defeat your enemies!" Sharif called, and people up and down the steep hills began to cheer. Heads popped out of darkened windows. Shutters were flung open, and men and women answered Sharif's call at the tops of their lungs. Before long, he saw brightly robed merchants and viziers rushing into the streets.

Several aeglors flew down, trying to drive the citizens back, to keep them under control, but they failed miserably. The oppressed people of Irrakesh threw stones and pottery, hot cooking oil, walking sticks, makeshift spears, and knives. The winged captors shouted out a war cry, demanding assistance.

The people swarmed out into the streets to defend themselves, to take back Irrakesh, and Sharif was amazed at how well they succeeded.

Piri blazed with a proud white light. Sharif laughed, wondering what would happen when Azric saw his plans crumbling. He cruised upward on the purple flying carpet to get a better view of the beautiful and intricate flying city. *His* city.

With a loud roar, something hurtled down toward him.

Instinctively he ducked to one side and a studded club whistled through the air, missing his head by no more than the thickness of his little finger. Sprawled on the purple rug, he looked up to see the aeglor leader back-flapping his wings, a weapon in each taloned hand and diving back toward Sharif for a second attack.

"Irrakesh is my city now," King Raathun bellowed.

With powerful strokes of his feathered wings, he plunged. Sharif sat up and took up his curved sword. Raathun swung his club, which Sharif ducked. The sword slashed down, but Sharif met it with his own. The weapons of the two flying monarchs clashed. Attempting to control the rug while defending himself, Sharif made it dodge to one side, then the other, racing away from the edge of Irrakesh and out to the open sea.

Sky fireworks erupted all around them as Lyssandra's father shot his casks of explosive powder into the air. When the aeglor king flew down, swinging his sword again, Sharif timed his counterstroke just right and struck backward, hitting Raathun's wrist with the curved blade. In surprise, the flying warrior dropped his blade. Blood ran down the aeglor's forearm and his sword spun, glittering like a silver ribbon as it tumbled far, far below to where the merlons were fighting in the sea.

Furious, Raathun flapped his wings and put on a burst of speed that even the flying carpet couldn't match. Using his injured hand and his momentum, he grabbed Sharif by the shoulder and yanked him off his carpet. Sharif struggled to raise his sword arm, but before he could, the big muscled aeglor gave a mighty heave and hurled Sharif out into the open air with a long, long fall below.

Sharif gasped, unable to cry out. He fell, the cold wind ripping past him. The churning battle below among sharks, merlons, remaining sea serpents, and Elantyans was frightening. Even more terrifying was the knowledge that, from this height, the impact of his fall to the ocean would kill him. Piri soared in, a streak of light in female form that crackled with angry lightning. When Raathun laughed in triumph, holding his club high with his bleeding hand, Piri unleashed a wave of power. Flaring like lightning bolts, bursts of electricity burned off Raathun's feathers, snapped his wings, and left the big warrior to tumble out of the sky, crying out in fury and shock. He fell like a stone.

Sharif was still falling, too. Piri kept pace with him, but he knew that as a ball of energy, she was too insubstantial to catch him. He had something he could do, however. Using the summoning rune embroidered into his carpet, he called it to him. As he fell through the air, getting closer to the waves each second, he hoped his carpet could react swiftly enough.

Raathun tumbled and spun, falling as fast as Sharif. Piri streaked away. Sharif reached out a hand toward her, but she was gone. The waves were coming up fast. He saw Barak's merlons and creatures clashing against the rebel merlons. No one seemed to have noticed them falling from the skies. Knowing he was going to hit, Sharif braced himself, though he knew it could do no good.

With a swiftness it had never before demonstrated, the flying carpet zoomed under him, with Piri at the helm. Matching his speed, the rug caught him like a soft, cradling hand and whisked him along, low to the surface of the waves at first, then gradually gaining height. Sharif panted, barely able to believe he was still alive, saved by his carpet and Piri.

A second later, Raathun splashed down on his back in the water, the impact slightly broken by his burned wings.

Looking back, Sharif saw that, though stunned, Raathun was not dead. He had, however, landed in the midst of the blood-maddened sharks the merlons had brought to the battlefield. The aeglor thrashed in the water, trying to straighten his wings and remain afloat. From his flying carpet, Sharif saw the sharks circle in. Raathun noticed them as well and shouted to the merlon king, demanding help.

No one listened.

The sharks, unable to distinguish between friend or foe, thinking only of gorging themselves in a feast, dove in and tore at the winged man. Sharif caught a last glimpse of the king of the aeglors, still thrashing, sinking beneath the waves in a cloud of red water.

CHAPTER 32

The last of the flying piranhas had been driven away or killed. The *Thunder Shield* had barely survived, its sails in tatters, its hull and deck damaged. But Vir Questas ordered the fleet forward on their attack. Several of the dripping, rotten ghost ships had been returned to their watery graves. Gwen had seen Vic and Tiaret open a new crystal door that swallowed up the largest of the attacking merlon creatures, but the fanatical King Barak did not retreat. He screamed for his merlons to fight to the death for their cause, though he himself hung back on his towering sea serpent next to an increasingly agitated Goldskin.

From the algae-covered prow of the *Golden Walrus*, the hideously disfigured Orpheon cast spells and ordered the launch of more deadly lavaja projectiles. Gwen wondered how many he could possibly still have in the cargo hold of the once-sunken ship. Ulbar and his merlon rebels continued to fight. Orcas engaged the sharks that were goaded by Barak and his followers.

Skimming the waves on wide-winged jhantas, Ulbar and several others did battle with the nearest plesiosaur, tossing their horn-tipped spears into the monster's curved neck. Having seen djinnis overhead and the decimation of the enemy merlon soldiers below, Gwen hoped the tide of battle was indeed turning in their favor.

Another group of allies appeared and joined Ulbar and his rebels. Gwen looked down to see dozens of small bubletts, domed undersea craft that carried anemonites who had been freed from Barak's weapons labs. Waves of other anemonites also arrived riding giant lobsterlike kraega steeds. Though much smaller than any merlon, the anemonites and their kraegas were formidable in their numbers. They carried small weapons like tiny javelins, and quickly took on the remaining merlons, killing many. Scattering as the merlons fought back, the anemonites reconverged and continued to press against their aquatic enemies.

Questas ordered their galley forward, intent on ramming the *Golden Walrus*, but Gwen had another idea. "Do we still have some of Sage Groxas's sky fireworks aboard?"

"Yes, Gwenya, two casks."

"I think we should try launching them at the *Walrus*, strike its hull."

"Very well. It should cause some damage," Vir Questas agreed, quickly sending a neosage to fetch the small barrels filled with the special chemicals Groxas had created.

But Gwen was confident. "I think it'll cause more than just a little damage. Remember, Orpheon's got dozens of lavaja bombs in there."

"Ah." The Vir's eyes brightened.

"And if we ignite one of them, we ignite them all," Gwen finished.

Questas nodded. "Yes, that is much preferable to ramming the wreck."

Orpheon stood gesticulating wildly, summoning up spells, rallying the merlons who accompanied him aboard the ghost ship. One more lavaja projectile spat into the air, arcing high and sweeping downward until it smashed into a storehouse on Elantya, exploded, and brought the building down, setting it on fire.

"Hurry!" Gwen said. "We have little time."

She and the neosage worked with the launcher and changed the aim point so that the cask would fly directly toward the *Golden Walrus*. When Questas gave them a nod, they activated the ignition rune painted on the small barrel. As smoke and sparks began to sizzle, they launched the canister. It flew in a perfect arc toward the *Golden Walrus*.

Orpheon saw it hurtling toward the side of his ship, down by the cargo hold. Even from their distance, Gwen thought she could see the waxy, lumpy skin around his eyes stretch outward in astonishment. His mouth formed an O, before the canister struck and exploded.

For the briefest of instants, all that happened was some splintering of wet wood. Then the real detonations began. The lavaja bombs split open and, in a surge of violently released heat and light, triggered other explosions. And more ... and more. The *Golden Walrus* erupted in an incredible burst of flame. At the last instant, Gwen saw the misshapen Orpheon alter his appearance, transform his body.

She remembered how, when they had pursued him on Elantya, Rubicas's traitorous assistant had reached a cliff and transformed into the shape of a merlon before diving off the rocks into the crashing waves below. Now his body sprouted wings—stunted batlike appendages, but strong enough to lift him off the deck. He flapped furiously, rising into the air as the *Golden Walrus* continued to explode and burn.

"He's flying to Irrakesh. He'll get away." Gwen bit the edge of her lower lip. "Then again, if falling into deep lavaja wasn't enough to kill him, an exploding ship couldn't have done it."

She watched the shape-shifter work his way up toward the city with his stunted wings.

Seeing the last of his enormous ghost ships destroyed, having watched three battle krakens and many of his sea serpents vanish through a crystal door, King Barak was livid, practically foaming at the mouth as he screamed to his merlons to continue fighting. "Fight together. I am your *king*. I command you to destroy these land-dwellers."

But Ulbar and his rebels now significantly outnumbered Barak's fighters. Goldskin, his last general, was with the king, but they had few armies left to command. The female merlon general surveyed the rebels and the fighting Elantyans. She seemed unimpressed by Barak's management of his forces or by the supposed power of Azric in the sky overhead. Knowing Goldskin's bloodthirsty temperament, Gwen kept an eye on the vicious merlon general. She and Tiaret had fought her in a demonstration of weapons prowess underneath the sea.

Gwen also knew that Goldskin was ambitious and would have no particular loyalty to Barak, especially when his great schemes were failing. Barak practically shrieked now, so furious that his words were incomprehensible. Goldskin lifted her pointed trident and let her sea serpent drop back slightly from the crazed king's. Gwen gasped. Barak suspected nothing.

Thrusting her trident forward, Goldskin skewered the maddened king from behind and lifted the shaft of her trident, holding the squirming Barak up in the air. "I have killed the one who corrupted us," she shouted, her words directed mainly toward Ulbar and his rebels. "I have saved us—we need no longer continue this useless fighting."

The leopard-spotted sea serpent, now free of the relentless goading of the merlon king, twisted its long neck around and opened its jaws to snap at its tormentor. Goldskin was only too happy to oblige. While Barak still twitched and cursed, she thrust her trident, along with its squirming victim, into the sea serpent's yawning mouth. The serpent snapped its jaws shut, disposing of the trident shaft and Barak all in one gulp. It tossed its head, opening its gullet, and a large lump made its way down the scaly throat.

Goldskin cried out to all the merlons, "I am now the leader of Barak's army. The fighting is over."

The rebel merlons circled the confused attackers, who had endured enormous losses, seen their titanic monsters defeated, and then watched the assassination of their king. They didn't know what to do. Ulbar's rebels surrounded and disarmed them. Within moments, all the fighting in the ocean was over.

Gwen crossed her arms and said, "I don't believe Goldskin has really had a change of heart, but she does understand how to survive. In other words, she saw which way the wind was blowing and decided this was her best chance to live until the end of the day. Still, I'm not about to complain." She found she couldn't stop grinning.

Vir Questas turned the war galley and they headed toward the harbor, where a triumphant Vic, Tiaret, and Lyssandra were waiting.

CHAPTER 33

B y the time the five companions came together again
with the merlons entirely defeated and the terodax and
aeglors nearly wiped out, they knew it was up to them
to fight Azric. Ven Rubicas, the surviving Virs, and Dr. Pierce
rushed down to the harbor to help the injured and assess the
damage. On a hill overlooking the harbor, Vic quickly described
their adventures to Gwen and Sharif, complimenting Tiaret and
Lyssandra. The girl from Afirik agreed that they had all fought
bravely. Knowing that time was short, the friends discussed
their ideas on how to defeat Azric.

Looking up at Irrakesh, Sharif was the first to point out that
it was moving. "Azric is pushing the city forward."

Piri streaked around them, glowing orange with agitation. As
Irrakesh glided through the air, it seemed to rumble. Vic half
expected to hear powerful thrumming engines driving the
mountainous island along. Irrakesh glided the rest of the way
through the crystal door. The rear fringe of its rocky perimeter
passed out into the sky so that the uprooted metropolis cast a
shadow over all of Elantya.

"I don't like this at all," Gwen said.

"Sheesh, that's an understatement," Vic agreed.

Sharif unrolled his flying carpet. "I believe Azric is about to do something terrible. We must stop him."

"With Orpheon at his side again, he will be more confident," Lyssandra said.

"And ruthless," Tiaret added.

Vic didn't want to imagine what would be worse than the terrible damage the dark sage had already inflicted upon the island, but he knew Azric would come up with something. Sharif jumped onto his purple carpet.

Vic spread out the larger carpet that had belonged to the sultan. "We're in this together. If you're going to fight Azric and Orpheon, I'm coming with you."

Gwen climbed on beside Sharif. "We all have to."

"We are the Ring of Might for a reason," Tiaret said, joining Vic on the larger carpet. "We are the five. We must fight together and find new ways to use our powers, as Lyssandra said."

Lyssandra climbed onto the carpet with Vic and Tiaret. "The bonds of our magic are strengthened when we are together. This is right," she said.

Piri swooped down in a flash of light and lithe movement.

Vic looked down and saw his father waving from the shore. Vic cupped his hands around his mouth and shouted, "Don't worry about us. We'll take care of it."

"How exactly are we going to do that?" Gwen said.

Vic gave her an eyebrow shrug. "We discussed that, didn't we? Go now, details later."

As the carpets took off, Gwen held her xyridium pendant and, with great effort, opened a window on Irrakesh, and kept it visible in front of them all as they flew.

In the floating city, the people had risen up and were still flooding through the streets, taking back their buildings, throwing out the last of the aeglors. Azric and Orpheon, however, stood outside the giant palace. Irrakesh hovered, thrumming with power. The dark sage guided it over the Citadel, over Rubicas's laboratory and tower, over all the main buildings.

"Faster," Sharif said, working the embroidery magic on his flying carpet. Piri flew beside him.

"Oh, no," Gwen said, looking at the image of Azric with sudden dread. "I think I know what he's going to do."

After listening to the window, Lyssandra said, "His best plans to destroy Elantya have failed. He believes the simplest solution is ..." She swallowed hard.

Vic looked at her and drew in a sharp breath. "You've got to be kidding me."

Needing no interpretation, Sharif finished for Lyssandra. "He intends to drop Irrakesh directly on top of Elantya. He will destroy everything."

"Now that his armies have been defeated," Tiaret said, "he has nothing to lose. He will do it."

"No, he won't," Vic said. "We can't let him."

They were still well below Irrakesh when the images of Azric and Orpheon in the window flung their arms wide, levitated above the floor of the balcony on which they stood, and began chanting.

"They are speaking the ancient tongue," Lyssandra said. "I do not know all of the words, but the dark sages are working great evil."

"Get out your crystal daggers, if you have them. Be prepared for anything," Gwen warned.

Suddenly the sky above the two carpets began to fall—or, more precisely, the city that had been hovering above them. If

Irrakesh plummeted to the ground, every living person in the city above and the city below would die.

"Now!" Lyssandra cried.

In unison, almost without understanding what they were doing, the five members of the Ring of Might raised their arms high overhead, their hands outstretched toward Irrakesh. They did not need their daggers. Quicksilver streams of power flowed upward from them. Lightning crackled beneath the descending city. Piri zoomed in circles around the display of raw energy. Rippling currents of air formed a shimmering support under Irrakesh and heaved it back into place.

Then all was silence. To Vic's surprise, Gwen's window was still open, showing the frightened people of the city looking around with cautious hope.

Azric and Orpheon were on the palace balcony once again. Shackled and gagged, Vizier Jabir stood nearby.

Sharif and Vic urged the carpets up to the city. Piri was crackling with energy but clearly much weaker than she had been. As soon as they reached the balcony, Tiaret sprang onto it, holding her unbreakable teaching staff. Sharif and Vic skidded the carpets to a halt on the tiled floor.

Azric and Orpheon turned. The dark sage was smiling. "Good. I so wanted you here to see what will happen next. I take it you didn't approve of my most recent endeavor? Of course you didn't—I can see that my motives were unclear. I wanted to save Irrakesh, I really did, but it seemed the most sensible choice under the circumstances. I understand perfectly why you would object. Still, I can't allow such interference to go unpunished, can I? Elantya, of course, is the greatest obstruction to my plans. Therefore, it—and most of you—must be eliminated. You see my point?"

Orpheon made a squawking sound that Vic realized was some kind of a laugh.

Sharif went over to check on Jabir, while Vic focused on Azric and Orpheon.

Now Vic saw up close exactly how much damage submersion in the lavaja cracks had done to Orpheon. His skin was grayish in patches, reddened in others, lumpy and yet polished smooth as if wrapped in a covering of melted and burned plastic. His eyes looked milky and uneven, no longer where they were supposed to be. His entire skull must have softened like wax, then shifted and changed.

"Glad to see that the outside matches the inside now, Orpheon. I like the new look. It suits you."

Azric's henchman was enraged. "I could tear you limb from limb, shock you to the marrow of your bones with dark magic rather than let you all die in a cataclysm."

Azric glanced at him in annoyance. "Don't be petty. I see that I was wrong to imperil Irrakesh simply to destroy Elantya. Instead, I will call forth lavaja from deep beneath the sea in a great volcanic eruption. Once I've eliminated all of the sages, the remaining members of the Pentumvirate, and Elantya itself, nothing will stand between me and opening the sealed doors. I can unleash my deathless armies." He gave a sad smile. "I only wish you could all survive long enough to witness it, but alas, we cannot have everything." He raised his hands. Vic heard a rumbling far, far below.

"Wait!" Gwen cried. "We have something you want—something you need. You can't kill us."

"Oh, but I can—at least some of you. There are so many problems to solve."

"We can solve them for you," Gwen said. "Much faster. We'll make a bargain with you."

"No—we *won't*," Vic said.

His cousin shot him a whose-side-are-you-on look, her violet eyes blazing. "Yes, we will. Hear me out, Azric."

"Gwenya, stop! You cannot!" Lyssandra cried.

Orpheon glowered, his melted-wax face flowing into a mask of anger. "Do not let them trick you, Azric. They will never agree to help you. We proved that under the sea with the merlons."

Azric brushed aside the comment. "Am I so easily tricked by mere children?"

Orpheon snapped backward in shock. "No, Azric. You are undefeatable."

The dark sage turned his smooth face toward Gwen. "Now, then. You refused me many times before. You and your cousin have very strong powers."

"You want to get to the worlds where your armies live—you even tried to get Vic's mother to break a seal for you."

"Yes, but she defied me. Go on."

Nervous, Vic glanced around at his friends. Tiaret appeared angry. Sharif looked hopeful. Lyssandra's eyes swam with tears.

Gwen forged ahead. "If you spare our friends and Elantya and Irrakesh, Vic can open a doorway for you to any world you choose—create a new door, just as he made the one here in the sky."

Azric looked startled. Then a smile crept across his face. "Yes ... of course. Simple and elegant." He glanced at Jabir. "And I already have my own Master Key to use after that."

Gwen moved her hand as if flattening a piece of paper in the air in front of her. "Look. Your armies are waiting for your return." A window opened. In the noiseless image, countless thousands of armored soldiers were conducting battle drills in a field outside a massive fortress.

"You see?" Gwen said. "We can reunite you with them."

Vic saw that this was indeed one of the worlds that had been conquered and devastated by the powerful immortal warriors Azric had been hoping to reach. But through Lyssandra, they already knew that the dark sage's generals there were not happily waiting for Azric. They hated him for abandoning them. Azric had no idea that the celebration he had glimpsed through the window had ended with his deathless generals and warriors tearing the surrogate Azric to pieces.

Vic shook his head, trying to look resolute. "You can't make me do this, Gwen. I won't."

Tears trickled from Lyssandra's frightened cobalt eyes now. "Please, Viccus. To save us?" She put a hand on Vic's arm, and her voice dropped to a whisper. "For me?" Looking desperate, she turned toward Azric. "Yes, Viccus will open a doorway to your armies for you."

"You are certain you won't need to unseal a door—you will simply create a new one for me?" Azric said.

"That's right," Vic said. "*If* you promise not to kill my friends or drop Irrakesh on Elantya—because *that* would kill my parents, our friends, and thousands of other people in both cities."

Azric paced back and forth on the balcony, a calculating look in his mismatched eyes. Orpheon kneaded his hands together. "Do not trust them," he said.

"Once he opens a new crystal door," Azric said, as if Orpheon were simply slow on the uptake, "the sealed one becomes irrelevant. I have a Key to travel back and forth. You understand what kind of bargain you are making, children?"

Sharif said, "Could it be worse than letting my flying city be annihilated and Elantya destroyed? This way at least we have a chance. There is hope."

Azric straightened with delight. "Very well, then. I offer you a reprieve—for now. You understand that I may require more than one of my worlds to spare Irrakesh and Elantya permanently?"

Vic nodded. "I thought you might."

Orpheon leaned toward the sage. "Think, Azric—is it worth it? You've wanted to destroy Elantya for so long. It is in our grasp."

"There was never a question about my ultimate goal," Azric said. "Perhaps you do not understand me as well as you should." He turned to Vic, his ancient eyes avid with anticipation. "Go on, then. Open a new crystal doorway and reunite me with my immortal armies—and Orpheon, too."

Lyssandra wept softly with relief.

"It is not right." Raising her staff, Tiaret moved as if to stop Vic, but Azric pushed her back with a flick of his finger.

Standing close to the glowing window that showed the enemy fighters, Vic spread his hands and concentrated. His magic worked in an instant, sparkles forming a new crystal door in the air, a portal into a devastated, condemned world. He was offering Azric the culmination of a dream he had cherished for five thousand years.

The invisible fragments of air parted and suddenly they could hear a great roar, a resounding cry of ferocious voices and clatters of weapons. The heat and the smell pushed back out into the skies of Irrakesh. Azric took hold of Jabir's chain and pulled him toward the new door.

Vic thought of his beloved Elantya, where he knew so many people, where his father remained, where his mother lay trapped in ice coral. "Wait!" he said as Azric started to step through the door. "First, tell me how to thaw my mother. How do I break the ice coral spell?"

Azric gave him a smug look. "I want to help you, I really do." He raised his eyebrows. "Perhaps when you open the next world for me...?"

Vic's heart sank at this cruel jab, though he had expected nothing better from the dark sage.

He looked back at Gwen's window. Noticing the crystal door,

Azric's soldiers began to rush toward it, snarling. "Hurry," Gwen said. "They can't all come out here onto the balcony. It will collapse."

Orpheon balked. "I could stay here, Azric—rule Irrakesh while you gather your armies." Piri flashed her blindingly bright light, directing it into the faces of the dark sages.

As planned, Tiaret shoved Orpheon toward the crystal door. The rest of the five sprang into action, too. Together they pushed. Suddenly understanding that this had been their intention all along, Azric cried out and tried to cast a spell at them. But their powers linked to form a rippling shield of energy in the air. Piri knocked Vizier Jabir's chain from Azric's grasp just before a powerful blast of wind slammed into Azric and Orpheon, propelling them through the door. Tiaret was already working her magic.

The door shut. In the window image, they could already see the dark sage searching for a Key.

Sharif sealed the crystal door. The portal that Vic had just created was permanently and irrevocably closed.

Gwen allowed her window to remain open just long enough to let them see Azric and Orpheon face the immortal armies rushing toward them. At the last moment Azric seemed to realize that his generals were not there to welcome him with open arms. Then the image faded.

Sharif ran to help Jabir.

"Cool," Vic said.

Lyssandra chuckled.

Vic hugged her and grinned. "Remind me never to play poker with you. You're a pretty good actress."

"We all played our parts well," Tiaret said. "The weeping, however, was quite believable. This will make a fine chapter in the Great Epic."

Gwen gave an involuntary shudder. "It *was* a pretty risky plan."

"But it worked," Vic said.

"Especially when the Air Spirits added their power to ours," Sharif observed.

And suddenly the giant forms of Air Spirits appeared in the sky all around Irrakesh.

"Thank you for your help," Sharif said with amazement.

In a sweeping rush, like musical thunder, a chorus of Air Spirit voices replied, "You and Piri have shown us the true nature of friendship. You risked your life for her, and she for you. Our sacrifice was a small price to pay to save our beloved friends in Irrakesh and our new friends in Elantya."

Lyssandra raised her hands toward the Air Spirits. "We are honored to accept your friendship and to offer you ours in return."

Vic gave a satisfied sigh. "I hope we've seen the last of Azric."

"We cannot be certain of that," Lyssandra said.

"He *is* immortal," Jabir reminded them.

"So are those generals who hate him," Tiaret pointed out.

Gwen sighed with satisfaction. "I think all in all we made a good bargain."

Vic grinned. "Azric didn't."

Drawing a deep breath, Sharif looked across the sweeping vista of the flying city of Irrakesh and out at the Air Spirits hovering around it. "The battle may be over, but our hard work is just beginning." Piri twirled over his head, shedding a warm yellow glow.

CHAPTER 34

The Ven Sages' laboratory chambers were quiet the next morning. All of the sages and students from the Citadel who had been working feverishly on defense projects for Sages Rubicas, Polup, and Pierce were now assigned to restoration crews wherever Azric and his armies had done the most damage. The Air Spirits were helping Jabir in Irrakesh.

Vic wasn't sure what he had expected in the wake of the great battles, but it wasn't this. Standing with his father, cousin, and friends in the peaceful alcove to which his mother's tank had been moved, he struggled against a painful tightness in his chest. A ray of sunlight touched the ice coral that encased his mother, giving it a faint ethereal radiance. Gwen gave his shoulder a light punch of sympathy before letting Sharif take her hand to comfort her. Vic glanced up when his father put an arm around his shoulders, but the look of anguished yearning on his face was too difficult to bear.

Vic forced words past the knot in his throat. "I guess I hoped that once Azric was defeated and gone, all the spells he had cast would disappear with him."

Lyssandra moved to stand beside Vic and placed a hand on his arm. "Our enchantments do not work thus." She slid her hand down to his, and he clasped it, letting himself draw strength from her.

"No offense, but we don't really know *how* this enchantment works, do we?"

Tiaret gave the marble floor a faint tap with her teaching staff. "Azric's power has grown for thousands of years, fueled by his greed for glory and power. What can match that?"

"Hmm. Yes, precisely," Ven Rubicas said, entering the alcove. "And yet you five, the Ring of Might, succeeded in thwarting him and trapping him in another world. How is it that you managed to do that?"

Sharif put his arm around Gwen's waist. "We share a bond." Hovering above his shoulder, the feminine energy ball that was Piri glowed a rich, earnest blue.

"We are willing to sacrifice our lives for one another," Tiaret said.

"Understanding," Lyssandra offered.

"Friendship," Vic added.

"*Love,*" Gwen said firmly.

"That's a sort of magic, isn't it?" Vic's father said.

Glowing turquoise with excitement, Piri did a pirouette above Kyara's tank, bathing it in a brightness that mere sunlight could not match. "Yes," Piri said aloud for all to hear. "Magic."

Sharif's fellow apprentices gasped with delighted surprise as Piri continued.

"Bonds. Sacrifice. Understanding. Friendship. Love." She twirled again. "*Magic.*"

"Our Air Spirit friend is quite correct," Rubicas said, tugging on his beard. "Together you all drew on powers that more than matched those that the dark sage brought to bear. I believe you already possess all the power you need."

"But *how?*" Gwen said.

With his free hand, Vic touched the xyridium pendant that hung at his throat. "Just like we did when we forged the Ring, and when we kept Irrakesh from falling."

Dr. Pierce nodded. "You drew on the magic and let it guide you."

"In other words," Gwen said, "we didn't know how, but we did what had to be done, anyway."

"Yup," Vic said. "So let's get started."

With a smile, the Ven Sage murmured, "*S'ibah.*"

His father plunged one hand into the water, as if to pull Kyara out the moment it became possible.

Even before the members of the Ring all joined hands, the designs on Vic's and Gwen's pendants began to glow, and the disks of xyridium rose into the air to hover parallel to the floor. As the Ring of Might concentrated, lightning bolts of power flashed back and forth among them. A faint answering glow emanated from the xyridium pendant worn by Kyara Pierce.

"Yes," Vic heard his father whisper. "It's working."

"*S'ibah,*" Rubicas murmured again.

Hovering above the tank, Piri shone with a powerful white light.

The random bolts of energy in the Ring became coherent, focusing into a single thick beam, and shot down into the tank, obscuring the ice coral in a light so bright they all instinctively squeezed their eyes shut. The flow of energy built and built until, with a roar like a mountain collapsing, it was suddenly gone.

Vic blinked his eyes open. Multicolored sparkles rained down through the air like a haze of rainbow static. When it cleared a moment later, the tank was gone—the crystal walls, the sea water, the ice coral. Only Vic's mother remained, lying peacefully on the floor of the alcove.

Cap Pierce dropped to his knees beside his wife's motionless form and kissed her lips. Color began to seep back into her pale cheeks, and her eyelids fluttered.

Elation cascaded through Vic in a dizzying torrent as his father helped his mother sit up. She raised a hand to touch her husband's cheek. "My love ..."

Vic couldn't wait any longer. "Mom!"

He threw himself down on the floor beside his parents and threw his arms around them. Seconds later, Gwen was on the floor with them, too, and they were all talking and laughing and crying, their words overlapping in a happy tumult.

Vic felt something press into his hand. He looked at the object: Lyssandra's magical vial of greenstepe. With a rush of gratitude, he offered the restorative to his mother, who drank deeply of it. When Vic glanced up to thank Lyssandra, he saw that Ven Rubicas, Tiaret, Sharif, and Lyssandra were withdrawing from the alcove to give the reunited family some time alone. But he could tell from the expression on the telepathic girl's face that she had already read his gratitude when she touched his hand.

Looking again at his father, mother, and cousin, Vic knew he had a great deal to be thankful for. He hugged them all again.

CHAPTER 35

The next day, the throne room in the Palace of Irrakesh overflowed with friends, dignitaries, and other well-wishers. Crowds filled the square outside below the balcony.

At Sharif's request, Ven Rubicas read a spell that projected images of the throne room into the sky above Irrakesh and over the island of Elantya, so that all could share in the festivities.

On the dais, scarred but much recovered, Jabir stood to the right of the throne, while Piri, radiating a glow of pride, hovered to the left of it.

From the steps at the base of the dais, Sharif surveyed the room. The prince had dressed simply yet elegantly for the occasion. Today he had chosen not to wear his customary billowy shirt. Instead, he had opted for an ivory satin vest embroidered with gold thread, a pair of cream silk pantaloons, and a gold sash. The open vest left his arms bare so that the brand he had received in merlon captivity was visible.

For him, the brand had become a symbol of how he had come to value hard work, sacrifice, friendship, and privilege. He no longer took his position in Irrakesh for granted. His job was not to be pampered and adored by his people. His job was to protect them from enemies and to serve them. As a token of his understanding that he must serve as well as lead, he had left his feet bare.

On the dais behind him, his closest friends honored Sharif with their support at this momentous event. Vic, Gwen, Lyssandra, and Tiaret were arranged near Jabir to the right of the throne, and Sharif had allowed Tiaret to carry her teaching staff. To the left of the throne with Piri were Ven Rubicas, the three remaining Virs, and Ulbar. The front row in the audience chamber was filled with sages, including Snigmythya, Abakas, Groxas and Kaisa, Polup, and Cap and Kyara Pierce.

A band of the finest minstrels from Irrakesh played joyous music. Sharif raised a hand of greeting to his guests, and the trumpeters played a fanfare as his valiant purple carpet, resplendent with new gold tassels, sailed into the room through the balcony entrance. Fluttering with pride, the flying carpet circled the chamber three times, swooped toward the dais, and settled itself neatly on the final few steps leading up to the throne.

At another fanfare from the trumpets, Sharif bowed, then turned and climbed the stairs to the seat his father had once occupied. To the cheers of the gathered crowd, he sat on the throne.

Jabir stepped forward and said, "I present to you, His Majesty Ali el Sharif, Sultan of Irrakesh."

Sharif found himself uncomfortable with all the applause, and after a few moments he held up his hands for silence. "Thank you for your good wishes. I only hope to prove myself worthy of your trust. And now, there is even more to celebrate." He motioned for Virs Etherya, Questas, and Pecunyas to come forward. "The people of this world, both Elantya"—he gestured to the Virs—"and Szishh"—he indicated Ulbar—"have invited

Irrakesh to stay here and become part of an alliance of sea, land, and air. No payments have exchanged hands. This is an alliance of equals, all of whom have sworn to uphold their duty to protect the worlds of the crystal doors. I have accepted both the invitation and the alliance."

A murmur of surprise and approval rippled through the crowd. Someone shouted, "But what of the Air Spirits?"

In answer, Piri twirled and announced in a musical voice that seemed to carry throughout the city, "We approve."

Sharif said, "The Air Spirits agree that the cause of protecting the worlds is noble. They say they can visit us in this sky as easily as another. And my dear friend Piri has consented to stay with me as their ambassador." The cheers grew deafening. The new sultan waited until they died down again. "The Virs of Elantya have good news to share, as well."

Now Etherya raised her voice and spoke to the crowd. "The people of Irrakesh, Szishh, and Elantya suffered many losses at the hands of Azric and his followers." The listeners became quiet and solemn. "Not the least of these was the death of Vir Helassa and Vir Parsimanias. But today is a day of joy, and it is with great pleasure that we tell you that Sage Polup has agreed to become our Vir of Resources, and Admiral Bradsinoreus will be our Vir of Protection."

The admiral, dressed in a red robe, and the anemonite sage in his clanking walker, came forward to join the other Virs on the dais. The crowd shouted its approval to see the Pentumvirate whole again.

"In addition," Etherya said, "Ulbar will represent the merlons as ambassador to the alliance. Ven Rubicas will lead the Council of Allies. Piri speaks for the Air Spirits, Jabir will represent Irrakesh, and the Sage Pierce has agreed to speak for the interests of outside worlds. Lastly, we owe much gratitude to the Ring of Might for their help in conquering the dark sage

Azric." Everyone listening, whether from sea, land, or air cheered. "The Ring, along with the Pentumvirate and Council of Allies will dedicate themselves to preserving peace for us all."

Etherya stepped back, and Sharif stood from his throne. "And now," he said, sweeping his gaze around the room, "we have more to celebrate than we can possibly name. Let us begin." With that, he turned to his friends and, without ceremony, gave each of them a hug while the excited crowds began to disperse.

The festivities lasted far into the night. Sage Kaisa had organized feasts for all members of the alliance, and Sage Groxas and Vir Polup put on a show of pyrotechnic magic.

The display alternated from land to sea to air and was unprecedented in its complexity and beauty.

Watching the fireworks from the balcony of the palace with his friends, Sharif caught glimpses of the Air Spirits dancing in the sky around Irrakesh.

CHAPTER 36

T he following afternoon, Gwen, Vic, and their friends slipped away together to the seclusion of a quiet cove, where they swam. Piri splashed and played in the water with them.

Afterward they sat on the beach, looking out to sea, enjoying the time just to be themselves. Here, where no one was watching them, they were not powerful members of the Ring of Might, an Air Spirit, or a sultan. Here they were just friends.

Sharif and Gwen held hands.

Putting one arm around Lyssandra, Vic asked, "Do you suppose that's it? The end of the prophecies?"

Lyssandra looked happier and more relaxed than Gwen could ever remember seeing her. "No. I still have dreams," the petite girl said. "And there are other prophecies here in Elantya."

"Oh, did we mention that we're going home?" Vic said.

Piri flashed orange with alarm, and at the look of dismay on their friends' faces, Gwen said, "Just for a visit. Uncle Cap and Aunt Kyara thought it would be a good idea. First," she put up her index finger, "we need to reassure the people who think we just disappeared. Second, we have to tie up some loose ends, like selling the house. Our neighbor Dr. Alami will probably take care of that for us. And third"—she held up three fingers —"we want to say goodbye to our friends and let them know that we're moving."

"Yup. To Elantya," Vic said. "Dad thinks we should tell them that we're going with Mom and Dad while they study an ancient culture in a place that's so remote that we'll be out of touch— maybe for years."

Gwen smiled at the look of concern that Sharif still wore. She hugged him. "Don't worry. We should only be gone a week or so."

"And then?" Lyssandra wanted to know.

Vic kissed her cheek. "Then we'll be back. We all have some pretty big responsibilities now, you know."

Tiaret got to her feet and gave each of the cousins a hug. Holding her staff, she looked toward the horizon, while Piri, flickering pink, drifted in lazy circles around the friends. "Do you believe the battle we fought was the prophesied final battle?" the girl from Afirik asked. "I have already begun to write that chapter for the Great Epic."

Lyssandra rested her head on Vic's shoulder. "I do not believe so."

"After all," Vic said, "Azric's still alive, isn't he?"

Sharif smiled. "As my people say: Accept each small victory, for there will be other battles."

A warm salty breeze ruffled Gwen's blond hair as she stared across the ocean with a sense of hope and excitement. "I think all of us still have a lot of adventures to come."

ACKNOWLEDGMENTS

We'd like to express our special appreciation to John Silbersack and Robert Gottlieb of the Trident Media Group for supporting this project from the beginning.

Jennifer Hunt & T.S. Ferguson for their enthusiasm and insightful editing.

Diane E. Jones and Louis Moesta of WordFire, Inc., for their invaluable comments; Catherine Sidor for her transcription; Timothy Duren Jones, Paul & Lacy Pfeifer, Jonathan Cowan, and D. Louise Moesta of WordFire, Inc.; and Kim Herbert of Herbert Properties, LLC, for keeping things running smoothly in the office.

Our families for putting up with our eccentric schedules and for introducing so many new people to our books.

Sheila Unwin for her wonderful teacher's guide materials.

Mike "Uncle Mike" Anderson for his work on our websites.

Sarah & Dan Hoyt, Rebecca & Alan Lickiss, Sean Moorhead, Bette Williams & Jack Moorhead, Eli "Skip" & Fran Shayotovich, Mohammed & Laila Alami, and Nora Alami for local cheerleading. Susan Bragg for getting us organized.

Kristine Kathryn Rusch, Dean Wesley Smith, Debra Ray, Lisa Chrisman, Max & Erwin Bush, Letha Burchard, Janet Berliner & Bob Fleck, Beth Gwinn, Janet Young & Michael Lee, Leslie Lauderdale, Katie Tyree, and Ann Neumann for decades of long-distance encouragement and keeping us sane in an insane world.

Harlan & Susan Ellison, Bob Eggleton & Marianne Plumridge Eggleton, Terry & Judine Brooks, Dave & Mary Wolverton, Dave & Denise Dorman, Dean & Gerda Koontz, Stephen & Jamie Warren Youll, Neil Peart & Carrie Nuttall, and Steven L. Sears for being brilliant and inspirational.

Cherie Buchheim, Mary Thomson, Len & Jill McLeod, Harry "Doc" Kloor & Rayna Napali, Linda Zaruches, and Michael David Ward for buoying up our spirits when needed, and for making us feel special.

Brian & Jan Herbert, Ron & Penny Merritt, Byron Merritt, Denise Jacobs, Liz Kettle, June Scobee Rodgers, Bill Styles, Megie Clarke, Cathy Bowden, Kelly Adams, Shannon & Linda Lifchez, Sandra Childress, Jim Briggs, Pat Tallman, Maryelizabeth Hart & Jeff Mariotte, and Brad & Sue Sinor, for their friendship and support.

ABOUT THE AUTHORS

Rebecca Moesta (pronounced MESS-tuh) is the bestselling author of forty books, both solo and in collaboration with her husband, Kevin J. Anderson. Her solo work includes *Buffy the Vampire Slayer* and Junior Jedi Knights novels, short stories, articles, ghost writing, and editing anthologies. She wrote the novelization for the Hallmark Channel Christmas movie *A Christmas to Remember*. With Kevin, she has written the Star Challengers trilogy, the Young Jedi Knights series, movie and game novelizations, lyrics for rock CDs, graphic novels, pop-up books, and writing books, such as *Million Dollar Professionalism for Writers* and *Writing as a Team Sport*.

Kevin J. Anderson is the author of 170 novels, 57 of which have appeared on national or international bestseller lists; he has over 23 million books in print in thirty languages. Anderson has coauthored fourteen books in the Dune saga with Brian Herbert, over 50 books for Lucasfilm in the Star Wars universe. He has written for the *X-Files*, *Star Trek*, *Batman*, and *Superman*, and many other popular franchises. For his solo work, he's written the epic SF series, The Saga of Seven Suns, a sweeping nautical fantasy trilogy, Terra Incognita, accompanied by two progressive rock CDs (which he wrote and produced). He has written two steampunk novels, *Clockwork Angels* and *Clockwork Lives*, with legendary drummer and lyricist Neil Peart from the band Rush. He also created the popular humorous horror series featuring Dan Shamble, Zombie P.I., and has written eight high-tech thrillers with Colonel Doug Beason.

Anderson and Moesta have lived in Colorado for more than 20 years. Anderson has climbed all of the mountains over 14,000 ft. high in the state, and he has also hiked the 500-mile Colorado Trail. Together, they are the publishers of WordFire Press.

IF YOU LIKED ...

If you liked *Crystal Doors: Sky Realm*, you might also enjoy:

Captain Nemo
by Kevin J. Anderson

The Magic Touch
by Jody Lynn Nye

Gunslinger: The Dragon of Yellowstone
by Ed Knight

OTHER WORDFIRE PRESS TITLES BY REBECCA MOESTA & KEVIN J. ANDERSON

By Rebecca Moesta & Kevin J. Anderson

Collaborators
Million Dollar Professionalism for the Writer
Writing As a Team Sport

The Star Challengers Series
Star Challengers #1: Moonbase Crisis
Star Challengers #2: Space Station Crisis
Star Challengers #3: Asteroid Crisis

By Kevin J. Anderson
Alternitech

Blindfold

Captain Nemo

Climbing Olympus

Clockwork Angels: The Comic Scripts

Dan Shamble, Zombie PI Series

Dan Shamble, Zombie P.I., 1: Death Warmed Over

Dan Shamble, Zombie P.I., 2: Unnatural Acts

Dan Shamble, Zombie P.I., 3: Hair Raising

Dan Shamble, Zombie P.I., 4: Slimy Underbelly

Dan Shamble, Zombie P.I., 5: Tastes Like Chicken

Working Stiff: The Cases of Dan Shamble, Zombie P.I.

Services Rendered: The Cases of Dan Shamble, Zombie P.I.

Hopscotch

Mr. Wells & the Martians

Resurrection, Inc.

The Saga of Seven Suns, Veiled Alliances

Short Story Collections

Selected Stories: Science Fiction, Volume 1

Selected Stories: Science Fiction, Volume 2

Selected Stories: Fantasy

Selected Stories: Horror and Dark Fantasy

Kevin J. Anderson & Neil Peart

Clockwork Angels

Clockwork Lives

Drumbeats

Our list of other WordFire Press authors and titles is always growing. To find out more and to see our selection of titles, visit us at:
wordfirepress.com

facebook.com/WordfireIncWordfirePress
twitter.com/WordFirePress
instagram.com/WordFirePress
bookbub.com/profile/4109784512